FIRE FATED

SHADOW PACK LEGENDS

LUNA M. ROSE

BUTTON PRESS

CHAPTER
ONE

I hit the ground with a dull thud, my boots sinking into the dirt. The heat was oppressive, even at this distance, and the smoke burned my throat the second I breathed in. My helmet strap hung loose against my chin, and I yanked it tighter, my hands trembling. I didn't have time for shaky hands. Not when Erin was out there.

This whole sneaking into one of the trailers while the firefighters were leaving Kitimat thing was starting to look like a terrible idea. Well, it had taken a turn about two hours ago on the highway when all we could see ahead of us was a wall of thick black smoke rising into the sky like a tidal wave.

The crackle of the fire roared in my ears, drowning out everything else. The wind shifted, and through the thick haze, the massive redwoods flickered in and out of sight like ghosts. The air vibrated with the chaos of the fire crew—clanging metal, shouted orders, the whine of radios. I tried to make myself smaller, ducking my head as I moved.

We never should have done this.

At least there had been extra gear for us to snag and fit in. Liam dropped down beside me, his landing silent, practiced. He looked infuriatingly calm, his uniform still crisp, helmet perfectly aligned, like we weren't standing in the middle of a disaster we had *no business being in.* Unlike me, his breathing was even, measured.

He scanned the scene, taking everything in. I doubted he had any better idea of what the crew was doing than I did. They unloaded tools and equipment, all of them working like a well-oiled machine, but we weren't near the fire itself. It was childish, but somehow I'd imagined them hooking up hoses or passing buckets of water.

Liam motioned to the left. We needed to move. We needed to disappear before anyone asked why the hell two pathetic looking firefighters had just stepped off the truck.

My gut twisted. We'd gotten onto it easily enough, slipping into the lineup of exhausted crews heading to the site, but now that we were here, *this* was the part that terrified me. We weren't supposed to be here. And if we got caught—if the pack found out—

No. We had bigger problems right now. Erin was out there. Alone. And I was balking.

I turned slightly, my dark ponytail pressed into the back of my head by the helmet. I bit my lip and gave him a sharp nod. We moved together, slipping through the chaos, ducking between trucks and equipment. I pulled my pack higher on my shoulder, the hastily gathered supplies inside jostling. We'd barely had time to throw together extra clothes before we ran. Once we shifted, we couldn't risk running back to the truck for them later.

The air thickened, the smoke curling around us, clinging to my skin, my clothes, my lungs. I fought the urge to cough, focusing instead on Liam's silent movements ahead of me. We reached the edge of the clearing, ducking behind a trailer when we found a cluster of firefighters stood a few feet away, heads bent over a map spread across the hood of a truck.

I kept my gaze down, hoping the dim light and the haze would keep us unrecognizable. My pulse hammered as we slipped past them unnoticed. *What if Erin's already dead?* I sucked in a slow breath, willing the thought away. No. She wasn't. She couldn't be. I wasn't going to let that happen.

Liam glanced back, his sharp gaze catching mine for just a second. I nodded. *Keep moving.*

I clutched my pack tighter. We needed to make this fast. I wasn't going to risk shifting here, not with this many eyes and radios crackling to life every few seconds, but that was our best bet of covering enough distance to get close to where Erin said she was last. All I had was the mention of the lake. There were plenty to choose from, but not many rogues were known to settle down. All I had to go on was a gut feeling.

Liam stopped abruptly, raising his hand. I froze, pressing myself against the side of a trailer.

A radio squawked somewhere to my right, a voice cutting through the haze. I held my breath, heart racing.

I tried to focus on the present. Tried to push past the fear clawing at my ribs. But my mind wouldn't cooperate. I imagined the trees already burning. I could see it—flames swallowing the trunks, glowing embers floating through the air like fireflies. For a second, I wasn't here anymore.

I was seventeen.

I was standing in the middle of another blaze, my heart hammering as flames roared all around me. The smoke had been so thick I could barely breathe, my lungs burning with every gasping inhale. The fire had been a living thing, ravenous and merciless, devouring everything in its path.

And then, the screams.

I clenched my fists, nails digging into my palms, but it was too late. The memories surged forward like a rising tide, unstoppable.

"Go! I have to help them, Mia! I can't just stand here and watch!" My mother's voice rang in my ears, clear as if she were standing beside me.

I remembered the way she had dropped to her knees beside an injured human, the man's breath coming in short, labored pants. He was barely conscious, his arms and legs blistered and raw, skin cracked open from the flames. His eyes had rolled up, his lips parted as he rasped something I couldn't hear.

I froze, my instincts screaming for me to pull her away, to drag her back to safety. But my mother had only looked at me, her dark eyes filled with something I hadn't understood at the time. A quiet kind of defiance. The same look Erin always had.

She pulled a tub from the pack on her back, rubbing it over the man's wounds while he groaned in agony. Then she laid her hands on the worst of it.

I watched, breathless, as a soft, golden light seeped from her fingers, spreading across his burned flesh. The glow shimmered, growing brighter, and then—before my eyes—the burns began to calm. They didn't fade completely, but the man's chest sagged, his head dropping back as if he could finally draw a full breath.

She was a healer, and I'd seen her work miracles before. But her magic always had a cost. That day, I'd seen it instantly. The second she pulled her hands away, she wavered, her body swaying like she might collapse. She'd spent too much of herself. Given too much.

And I wasn't the only one who had seen.

I had barely managed to pull my mother away, half-carrying her, her body weak from the magic she had drained. The entire time, my mind had screamed with a single truth. We were dead.

And I hadn't been wrong.

The punishment had been swift. Brutal.

The pack's laws under Nathan Black were clear—no shifting near humans or public spaces and no compassion when it meant risk for the pack. Especially to she-wolves. Ironic, considering the stories Evelyn told me about his protective nature.

It didn't matter that my mother had saved lives. It didn't matter that she had been the best healer the pack had ever known. The alpha had made his ruling in front of everyone.

The heat that day had been stifling, the sun beating down as the pack gathered in the clearing. The silence had been the worst part. No one had spoken. No one had tried to stop it.

I had wanted to. I wanted to scream, to throw myself between my mother and the alpha, but Liam had gripped my wrist, holding me back. *Don't,* he had mouthed. *Please.*

I had been powerless to stop it.

I could still hear the crack of the whip as it struck her bare back, the sharp gasp she had let out on the first lash. By the third, she had stopped making a sound. By the tenth, she had collapsed, her body hanging limply from the ropes binding her wrists. And by the time they had finally let her go, the damage had already been done.

She had never been the same after that. She never fought like that again. Our family lost her forever.

It was after that moment—after Erin watched our mother break—that my sister had decided she was done. She had always been the reckless one, the one who pushed back against the rules, but that day had shattered whatever fragile ties she still had to the pack.

The night she left, I had begged her to stay. Erin was more than my sister, she was my other half. Even though we were born years apart, our magic connected at my birth. When Erin and I touch, our feelings and thoughts transfer—not in words, but in colors and meaning. Something neither of us has ever been able to explain. Losing her felt like inheriting a phantom limb.

For weeks and months I blamed her. But it hadn't taken long for me to realize the truth. She hadn't left me. By not standing up, not joining with her, I'd abandoned her that night. We all had. And I wasn't going to do it again.

A hand landed on my shoulder, and I flinched. "Hey." Liam's voice cut through the haze of my memories, pulling me back to the present. Right. Get the hell out of here.

I blinked, swallowing against the lump in my throat. "Sorry. I'm good."

Liam nodded once, then crouched, muscles coiled as he waited. I forced myself to stay still, ignoring the panic rising in my throat. Finally, Liam gave the all-clear. I exhaled sharply and followed.

We slipped between the last few trailers, moving fast now. I didn't let myself think about what would happen if we were caught. We wouldn't be. We *couldn't* be.

Ahead, the trees loomed dark against the ominous glow from the north. That was our window. If we could make it to the tree line, we could shift and move faster, find our way up to Bear.

But then, just as we were about to make a sprint for it, I saw it. Through the window of the last trailer.

I tugged on Liam's arm. "Hey, wait." He frowned, but I pointed to our right. "I think that's the data center."

"They have a data center?"

I shrugged. "I assume so. Maybe we could quickly look at the boundaries. Make sure we skirt them."

Liam gritted his teeth. He didn't like it, but he wasn't saying no. I crept up to the trailer, lifting to my tip toes and peering through the glass. "There's nobody in there."

Liam went first. I followed and we both slipped into the trailer, the door clicking shut behind us. The air inside was cooler, thick with the hum of machines, the dim glow of screens casting eerie shadows on the walls. My shoulders relaxed a fraction.

Finally, something going our way.

I didn't let myself savor it. Time was running out. I crossed the space in a few steps, my fingers brushing over maps, papers, and whatever the hell else they had laid out on the table. It was all a mess of symbols and numbers that made no sense to me, but at least I could understand the lines on the map.

"Here." I spread the stack of papers on the table, the ink rubbing on my fingers. The town names and rivers were familiar enough, but it was the thick red lines and jagged arrows that made my stomach churn.

"This is the fire perimeter, right?" I traced the border with my finger, the heat from outside making the paper feel warm under my touch.

Liam nodded, his voice tight. "Yeah."

My thoughts exactly. I had no idea how massive this thing was. I turned and stared at another map on my right. Arrows. That had to be predicted wind patterns or something since it clearly showed the fire moving south. "That's good news isn't it?" I ignored the fact that if the fire had already swept through Erin's area, it didn't matter how fast it moved away from her.

Liam grunted. "This is almost as good as when we tried to read the weather maps in Mrs. Haver's class."

My jaw dropped. "You remember that?"

"Hell yes I do. It was the only time I beat you on a test. You got a C."

"Hey, that was a solid C."

"Because you flirted with the TA."

I scoffed. "I did *not* flirt—"

Liam raised a knowing eyebrow. "You brought him cookies, Mia."

"They were for the whole class!"

"And yet, somehow, he was the only one who got two."

I rolled my eyes, but a small laugh escaped. It felt good, even for just a second. Then reality crashed back in. Liam must've felt it too, because the humor faded from his expression.

I swallowed hard and tapped my finger on the map. "The river. If we can't get through on the east, we could use the water."

Liam stepped closer, tracing the route with his finger. His expression sharpened with thought, working through the logistics. "We'd have to be fast. If the fire jumps too soon—"

"I like how we're pretending we know anything about this shit."

Liam snorted. "Your idea to enter the data center."

I ignored him. I couldn't very well take any of the computers or equipment, but I quickly snapped a few photos with my phone camera, then slung my pack over my shoulders and followed Liam to the front of the trailer.

Just as he was about to reach for the handle, the door shoved open with a creak, and my heart leaped into my throat. Liam stepped in front of me just as I caught a glimpse of broad shoulders and sandy hair coming up the steps.

I froze, clinging to Liam like a toddler. "What the hell are you doing here?"

CHAPTER

TWO

The trailer's metal door slammed against my back as I halted on the steps, sweat and smoke clinging to my skin. Mia. My daughter Elle's former babysitter. My mind stumbled, trying to reconcile the girl I remembered with the woman standing before me now. My daughter was almost twenty, which meant Mia had to be, what, twenty-four at least?

I recognized her instantly, but she was taller than I recalled. Her legs stretching in those tight jeans, the fabric hugging her in ways that made my chest tighten. Which only made me feel like the asshole when she was the one obviously trespassing. Her hair was tied back in a messy bun, strands escaping to frame her face. The hazy glow from the small window highlighted the sharp angles of her jaw, the way her lips parted slightly as she turned to face me.

Then her expression hardened. "Mr. Bast—"

"It's Connor," I snapped, my stomach roiling. *Mr. Bastien.* That was my father's name. She knew me as an adult—a dad. Like her parents. *Holy shit.* I went to run a hand through my hair, but I was still wearing my helmet.

"You know him?" the man beside her hissed. He was young. Strong. I assessed him out of habit. After years testing my crew, I couldn't help but categorize physicality. His smug expression made something inside me twist with irritation.

She nodded, looking like she'd tasted something bitter. "He's the fire chief in Kitimat."

Mia spat the title like a curse word. "Huh. Quite the endorsement." I had to admit, the disdain rolling off her intrigued me. I hadn't seen her in ten years and she'd broken into one of my trailers.

I forced myself not to notice the curve of her neck, the faint freckles across her cheeks. I felt a surge of heat in my bloodstream, a primal, gut-deep attraction that filled me with shame. She was younger than me, *years* younger, and I was in the middle of mitigating a crisis.

But honestly, that tracked. By the three donuts I'd eaten already that morning, my body was searching for an escape from the constant stress. I'd been stuck out here for three weeks, and there weren't many women in this camp. None that looked like her. That made sense. The more worrisome fact was that I'd always been drawn to women who treated me like shit.

I clenched my fists, my nails digging into my palms. "Start talking," I growled.

Mia flinched, something flickering in her eyes. But then she squared her shoulders, her chin lifting. "We were just—" she began, her voice steady despite the way her hands were trembling.

I didn't let her finish. "Don't lie to me, Mia," I snapped, the words tearing out of me before I could stop them. "You're not good at it."

Her gaze dropped, and I pushed away the pang of regret. They were in our damn data trailer. In a restricted area. They were going to get themselves killed.

When she didn't open her mouth, I let out an exasperated sigh and took off my hard hat, then climbed the steps to stand in front of them. Her friend, whoever he was, stood a head shorter than me. *Good.* I'd already struck the fear of God into them. I didn't need to make it worse. Plus, this was my only break in thirty-six hours. I didn't feel like fighting another battle.

My boots echoed on the aluminum floor, and I didn't need to say a word. They both straightened up like guilty kids caught stealing candy. "Sit," I barked, jerking my head toward the bench. My tone left no room for argument. Her friend's eyes narrowed, but he obeyed, flopping down with an arrogance that made me want to knock the smirk off his face. Mia hesitated, her hands twisting, before she finally sat beside him. The bench creaked under their combined weight.

I crossed my arms, planting myself in front of them like a barricade. "You're in a restricted zone. No trespassing signs are there for a reason."

Mia's eyes darted to her friend who shrugged, leaving her to take the lead. She opened her mouth, and again, I could see the lie forming on her tongue. "We were lost. We saw the fire and wanted to help. We didn't know this was a restricted area."

So. Now she was playing a woman in distress. I raised an eyebrow. "Lost? You don't get lost up here." I turned and peered through the window. "Plus, I don't see any unaccounted-for vehicles, and this one doesn't strike me as a biker."

I turned back and motioned to her friend's fitted jeans and pristine Air Force Ones.

Her gaze dropped, a blush rising to her cheeks. My ex-wife had looked like that when she lied. I'd always attributed it to something else, and it had taken me years to learn the difference, to recognize when someone was hiding the truth. But I'd gotten good at it. Too good.

I clenched my jaw. "You're putting yourselves and my crew at risk. Do you have any idea how dangerous this fire is?" Mia grimaced, but I pressed on. "It's spreading fast, fueled by dry timber and these bat-outta-hell winds. We're talking hectares burned, lives at risk. And you're out here playing hero without a clue?"

That fire flared in her eyes. "My sister. She lives up north. I haven't heard from her."

My shoulders dropped an inch. There it was. Something that made sense. "You should know better." The fire in Kitimat had ripped through our neighborhood. We'd lived three doors down from Mia's family. Elle had been at a friend's house. It was my first year on staff.

None of that explained her animosity. Our team had saved her house. She should have brought me a damn bundt cake.

Mia observed me, her eyes sharp. "Seems we're both gluttons for punishment."

My jaw tightened. Did she know about Lydia? About Elle? I doubted it. Mia had been our babysitter and I knew her parents, but after Lydia and I split up, I became a bit of a hermit.

She was probably talking about that night. About how Elle had barely made it out alive. Everyone in Kitimat knew that story. I relived it more nights than I could count.

I dragged a hand down my face, stuffing that memory down deep. If her sister was up north, I felt for her. My team had been fielding calls twenty-four-seven, but that didn't excuse irresponsible-ass behavior. "I understand that you're concerned, but the two of you need to get the hell home." The friend shot Mia a glance, and my brow furrowed. "How did you get here?" Mia opened her mouth, then closed it as I parsed out potential options. They couldn't have come via the main road since there were blockades. Our other fire teams were clear cutting and ripping up trenches from here to the highway.

I frowned and glanced at Mia. "Are you the biker?"

Mia's eyes widened, and she laughed in surprise. "No, I—" She shook her head. "No." When she looked up, the flush on her face had spread to her neck. Her jaw tightened as she folded her arms over her chest. "We snuck onto the trucks."

That was the truth. I didn't like it, but she wasn't lying. I cursed under my breath and turned, pacing to the other side of the trailer. The fire was spreading fast—forty thousand hectares and counting. The wind was shifting, carrying embers toward the dry east side of the forest. If it jumped the containment line, we were screwed. And here I was, wasting time babysitting.

I turned back to face them. "This isn't some small brush fire. This is a monster. It's already taken out three towns, and if the wind keeps pushing it, it'll be unstoppable. I can't spare any trucks to Uber you back to Kitimat."

Mia considered this. "Right. We'll get going—"

"Go where?" I threw out my hands. There weren't any towns within an hour of here that hadn't already gotten evacuation orders.

Her friend shrugged and stood. "I'll take care of it."

I couldn't help it. That made me grin. "She must be special if you're going to get those kicks dirty for her."

Mia stood next to him, her eyes flashing. "He's just a *friend*, and I forced him to come with me, so don't be an asshole."

Friend. She was defensive. Interesting.

My head started to pound. Probably from smoke inhalation. I needed to sleep. And I couldn't leave these two running amuck. "Walk. Now." I motioned toward the door of the trailer and started forward. Their shoes scraped against the floor.

"Connor—"

"I could have you arrested if that's easier?" I glanced back over my shoulder. Mia looked like she hadn't exhaled in a full minute. Honestly, if she passed out, this whole thing might be easier.

We stepped outside, and my eyes started to sting. Not that the air in the trailer was much better, but the filtration system must've been doing something.

Mia jogged up to match my stride, but she had to take two steps for every one of mine. "Liam has a friend who lives not far from here—"

"Oh yeah? What's the name?" I called back.

"Hazelton."

I nodded. "Evacuated them three days ago."

Mia pursed her lips and looked back over her shoulder. She nodded once. "They didn't evacuate."

I frowned. I didn't hear Liam say a word. "Well, then they're idiots, and you shouldn't go stay with them." I stopped and pulled on the door of my trailer, then opened it wide and motioned for them to go in.

They climbed the stairs and stood off to the side as I entered.

"Is this . . . ?" Mia trailed off.

I nodded. What the hell else was I supposed to do with them? "My trailer. You'll stay here for the night, and I don't want to hear any arguments."

CHAPTER

THREE

MIA

I stood close to Liam, taking in Connor's trailer. *Connor.* It was so weird calling him that. I saw other adults who I'd grown up with around town all the time, but he wasn't one of them. Somehow, he'd stayed frozen in time in my head.

Punch him out and we'll go, I sent to Liam.

Yeah. Based on what you told me, that wouldn't be a good idea.

I'd filled him in on the walk to the trailer. I gritted my teeth. *Then make it so he doesn't remember this.*

Liam shot me a look. *Yeah? You want me to kill him? Not exactly what I signed up for.*

I drew a breath and held it, watching Connor drop his gear. He had a short, well kept beard now, a little gray at the edge of his sideburns. He was bigger—thicker. My stomach churned as memories swirled through me.

He was the one who talked to Nathan Black.

Elle had been caught in the fire that night. She was over at a friend's house, stuck on the top floor with no way out. The firefighters had gone in. Connor was out of town, and they couldn't find Lydia. They pulled her out. Couldn't get her breathing again.

My parents, especially my mother, had been distraught. I watched them arguing in the kitchen. My father insisting my mother stay put, not meddle in human affairs. My mother arguing that our magic was useless if we didn't use it to help— to protect.

I was old enough to understand that when my mother walked out the door, she was in direct defiance of our alpha. When people in town started talking about Elle suddenly breathing again—about her lungs having no permanent damage—I knew what that meant, too. My mother was the pack healer.

When Connor Bastien came poking around, asking about a woman that was seen at the ambulance, it wasn't too hard for Nathan Black to put two and two together either. Connor Bastien didn't turn away when other members of the pack— including my father who worked at the school where Elle attended—told him he should leave it alone, and my mother had paid the price.

I didn't want to be here. I didn't want to look at his face for another second. But Liam was right. Given that Connor was connected with all the leadership in Kitimat, I couldn't give him another reason to get involved in pack affairs. While there was no chance Rowan would react the way Nathan had, that was exactly why I didn't want to make life harder for him. The humans had plenty of reasons to think we were strange, but no proof that we were more than eclectic. I wouldn't be the reason that changed. Not tonight.

Connor moved around the cluttered trailer. The space

seemed too small for a man with his frame. He hung his helmet on the small shelf with hooks behind the fold out table, then shrugged off his heavy coat.

Damn. He didn't have those arms before either. The navy blue shirt pulled taut over his broad shoulders and biceps. I dropped my eyes. Why were arrogant assholes always the hot ones?

We're not sleeping here. Liam's voice sounded in my head.

I jumped, then shot him a look. Of course we weren't sleeping here. But we also weren't going to cause a scene with the fire chief. *As soon as he sleeps, we'll leave, but I don't want this getting back to people in Kitimat,* I sent back.

Liam raised an eyebrow. *You don't think he's going to tell everyone you've been naughty?*

My cheeks flushed. I wanted to snap at him, but I had no right to do so. Liam deserved all the patience in the world after what he was having to deal with on my account.

I rubbed my hand, not even realizing I was doing it until Connor turned. The last thing I wanted was to draw more attention to it. I'd already caught him looking.

"I'm assuming you two are hungry." Connor yanked open the fridge and pulled out three individually packaged freezer meals.

"You don't have to—" I started, but the look he gave me shut me up. He seemed exhausted. Dark circles under his eyes. He wasn't with the other firefighters we saw at the station, which meant he must have been camped up here already.

Connor ripped off the plastic on the first meal and threw it in the microwave, typing in three minutes on the display. Then he turned, his eyes meeting mine, and for a moment, the world outside faded. My wolf lifted her head, staring straight at him with her hackles up.

Shh, down girl. I mentally stroked a hand over her head.

She'd been standing at attention since Connor busted us in the data center.

The crackle of the radio cut through the thick air of the trailer. "Bastien, you better be asleep already. You've been running on fumes for days." The voice was female and sharp.

Connor's jaw tightened as he pulled the walkie-talkie from his belt and adjusted the dials, his movements precise but weary.

"What is it Tiff," Connor replied.

"Nothing. Just me telling you to turn off the damn news and sleep."

Connor blew out a breath and hit the button. "Thanks, Mom."

Guilt wedged between my ribs, but I shoved it away with annoyance. I didn't need to feel bad for him. He probably got off on being the tough guy—the chief that never slept.

Another crackle. "Don't make me spank you."

My eyes widened as Connor looked up, chagrined. "That— she's kidding. She's my deputy fire chief."

I smirked, relishing the embarrassment written all over his face. "Don't worry, I won't tell HR."

He clicked the walkie-talkie back into it's holster and opened the microwave five seconds before it beeped. Grasping the edge of the packaging, he pulled the meal out and set it on the thin stretch of counter, then prepped the next meal and slid it in, hitting the buttons a second time.

"We're not sleeping together," he muttered when he turned back to face us.

I shrugged. "Wouldn't care if you were."

Connor held my eyes a moment too long, and my skin started to heat. When he finally turned back to the fridge, I let out a relieved breath. I didn't like when he looked at me.

"You know, I'm fine actually." I shoved my hands in my

pockets. "I'll just—" I set my pack on the floor next to me and curled my legs up on the bench. Maybe if I pretended to relax, Connor would go to bed himself and we could get out of here faster.

Connor handed Liam the first meal with a fork. As he peeled back the top, the scent of lemon chicken filled the trailer. My mouth watered.

"You sure?" Connor held up the last meal.

I nodded once, shooting a glare at Liam who took his first bite.

What? he asked through the bond.

We need him to go to his room faster so we can get out of here.

Liam blinked. *Right. I'll eat faster.*

I suppressed a groan.

You should probably stop staring. Liam put a forkful of chicken into his mouth.

I snapped my head toward him. *I wasn't staring.*

He grinned. *Defensive?*

Heat crawled up the sides of my neck. *There aren't many places in here to look.*

Right. Definitely observe his ass then.

I rolled my eyes and turned on the bench to face out the window. Had I been looking at his ass? Considering I knew Connor was wearing Levi's, probably. I ran my hand over the smooth laminate wood of the tabletop. It was shocking. His transformation. That was all.

"Something wrong?" Connor asked behind me.

I shook my head, not turning to look at him. Outside the light had faded, but there was still an orange glow painting the sky in the distance, hovering ominously over the silhouettes of the trees.

My bladder twinged as the microwave door opened, and I

turned. "Actually, do you have a bathroom somewhere? I could—"

"Right there." Connor pointed to a narrow door to my left. "It's not the Ritz, but it's clean."

Well, using the bathroom as an excuse to disappear wasn't going to work, but at least I could be comfortable. I grabbed my pack and stepped into the small bathroom, closing the door behind me.

The space was cramped, the air faintly scented of cinnamon. Connor's toiletries lined the counter with military precision—soap, toothbrush, deodorant. A small bottle of cologne sat in the corner, the label worn. He wore cologne all the way out here? Not sleeping together, my ass.

I pulled out my own toiletries, the familiar routine grounding me, until my eyes snagged, and I froze. That electric shaver. It was the same one he'd had on his bathroom counter in his house.

The memory hit me like a slap. It had to have been nearly ten years ago.

I'd barely gotten there to babysit Elle. Connor and his wife were getting ready upstairs. They were a young couple, cool. I thought his wife—Lydia?—was gorgeous with her long blond hair and curvy figure. She wore a low-cut red dress that night. I remembered because I could see her cleavage, and I wondered if she was wearing a push up bra. I instantly wanted one.

Elle was nine and I was fourteen, so it was a pretty easy gig. That night, though, I was only trying to keep her distracted.

I don't know when the argument started, but we'd heard their raised voices in the middle of our game of Go Fish. A few minutes later, Lydia stormed out the front door without a jacket, leaving the house tense and quiet. When I didn't see Connor appear, I went about our regular routine. Fed Elle dinner and played a few more card games. When I put her to bed, that razor was on the counter.

And that was the last time I was asked over.

I shook the memory away, my heart racing. The past had a bad habit of clawing its way back when I least expected it. I should know that by now.

I splashed water on my face, the coolness a welcome shock, then stared at myself in the mirror. When I finished in the bathroom, I rejoined Connor and Liam in the living space to find that Connor had already flipped the table to reveal the bed, and was now arranging the bench cushions into a makeshift mattress on the floor.

You let him make us beds? I growled at Liam.

Liam's jaw tensed. *At this point, you still think he's a man who can be reasoned with?*

I set my pack next to what had been the bench, but Connor stood and picked it up. "Hey—"

"You're in here." He passed me, brushing my arm, and any arguments died in my throat. He smelled good. That same warm spice I'd picked up in the bathroom mixed with campfire. Connor pulled back the curtains, revealing a queen bed that took up the whole back of the trailer.

"No." I shook my head. "Remember your girlfriend? You're supposed to be the one getting rest."

Connor's jaw tensed as he turned back to face me. "Call me old fashioned, but I don't let women sleep on my floor."

I scoffed. "Wow. How gallant of you." He didn't let women sleep on his floor but he'd refuse to listen to them and go behind their back to their alphas. I crossed my arms over my chest. "I'm not going to take your—" I gasped as Connor crossed the space in one long stride. His hands circled my waist, and he lifted me straight off the damn floor. "Connor!"

He dropped me on the bed, handed me my pack and

stepped back. "Goodnight." He closed the curtain, leaving me gaping like a fish.

Okay. I think I like him. Liam's laugh landed in my head.

Don't. I sat stewing on Connor's mattress, considering my next move. But what move was there? Connor was exhausted. Hopefully he'd sack out next to Liam in the next few minutes. *Tell me when it's safe.*

Will do. He's changing now. Do you want a play by play?

Liam, I swear—

Kidding. Don't get your panties in a twist.

I flopped back on the mattress, careful to keep my boots from touching his quilt. My panties were already twisted. Just not for any reason I was going to divulge to Liam.

My heart raced, and I sucked in a greedy breath. That whole thing Connor just did? It pissed me off. And I didn't think I'd ever been this turned on in my entire life.

I turned my head and frowned. Damn it, everything in here smelled like him.

Mia?

What?

Slight problem. Uh . . . your buddy Connor just locked the door from the inside and put the key in his pocket.

CHAPTER

FOUR

CONNOR

I lay on the narrow bed made of bench cushions, staring at the ceiling, the weight of my eyelids pulling me down, but my mind refusing to shut off. The fire wasn't just burning out there in the woods, it was chewing away at my insides too. I knew every minute counted, and here I was, wasting time trying to catch a few winks.

I sat up, the plastic creaking softly. Liam was sprawled on the table bed, his chest rising and falling with each breath. The rustling sounds behind the curtain had stopped at least thirty minutes ago. Either Mia was asleep or she was a ninja. Neither would surprise me at this point.

I stood and crept to the stairs, reaching for my boots first. The heavy leather creaked as I pulled them on. My Nomex shirt was stiff with dried sweat, but I didn't exactly have the option of going into my bedroom to change. I pulled on my coat,

24

grabbed my hard hat, and stepped outside, the cool night air pressing against my cheeks and forehead.

The camp was alive with activity, the glow of headlamps bobbing like fireflies in the dark. I spotted my crew gathered near the command post, their faces lit up by the faint light of tablets and radios. They turned as I approached.

"Connor," one of the guys called out, his voice hoarse from the smoke. "We've got a situation."

I nodded, my gaze scanning the group for Tiff. "What's the word?"

"The fire's moving faster than expected," Tiff stepped forward. Her sharp features were highlighted by the light of her headlamp, and her short blond hair was tied back in a tight ponytail. She was my deputy, and she didn't mince words. "The left flank is getting out of control. We need to get a line cut before it jumps the ridge."

I grunted. "You should've called me."

"You should've been sleeping." Tiff leveled her gaze at me.

I nodded, my mind already racing. "Alright, let's move. We'll start back burning along the ridge. I want a line dug from the creek to the old firebreak." I nodded to Tiff. "Hold down the fort."

"I always do." She saluted me, and turned back to the tent.

The team nodded, their faces set with determination. We knew the drill. This wasn't our first rodeo, and we'd been through worse. But this fire was different. It was hungry, unpredictable, and it wasn't going to go down without a fight.

We set off into the darkness, the only sound the crunch of gravel beneath our boots and the occasional crackle of the radio. The fire was ahead of us, a wall of orange and yellow that lit up the sky like a sick sunset. The heat even this far from the blaze was visible, making the air shimmer and dance.

The team sprang into action, their silhouettes stretching

long in the dim glow of headlights and the distant flicker of the fire. The flames weren't close—not yet—but the heat still pressed against us, a steady, unrelenting force in the dry night air. We were in the buffer zone, a few kilometers ahead of the fire line, where the goal wasn't to fight the flames directly but to clear everything burnable before they got here.

Our crew was strictly clear-cutting. Chainsaws snarled to life, the high-pitched wail of the engines rising and falling as trees toppled in controlled succession. The scent of fresh-cut pine mixed with the acrid bite of smoke hit sharp in my lungs despite the filtration of my mask. Further down the line, other crews worked on trenching and digging handlines, their Pulaskis and McLeods biting into the dirt, carving out barriers meant to stop the fire's advance.

I walked the line, my boots crunching through dry underbrush and sending up little puffs of dust and ash. The soil here was loose and thirsty, the drought having drained every ounce of moisture from the earth. Even with our cutting efforts, I knew it wouldn't take much—one ember, one gust of wind—for the fire to breach containment.

My radio crackled. "Connor, this is Tiff. Air tankers are overhead. Dropping retardant now. We're getting a solid perimeter, but we need to keep moving."

I grabbed the radio from my holster. "Copy that." My voice came out hoarse, my throat raw from the smoke even with a bandana over my face. I tucked the radio back, scanning the terrain as another tree crashed down to my right, the vibration humming through my boots.

Overhead, the tankers made their pass, their deep, guttural roar cutting through the night. A moment later, the thick, red stream of retardant sprayed out, falling like a bloody mist over the treetops ahead. It wouldn't stop the fire, but it would slow it, coat the vegetation, give us a chance to widen the break before the flames caught up.

We kept working, methodical and relentless. No one talked much. The only sounds were the chainsaws, short snaps of orders and instruction, and the distant white noise nobody would choose to go to bed to. The night stretched long, every motion mechanical, every swing of an axe or rev of a saw blending into the next.

I worked until my shoulders screamed for a break, then leaned against the fender of a dusty fire truck and yanked my canteen off my belt. The water was warm, but I didn't care. I took a long swig, and it trickled down my parched throat. My phone was in my hand before I realized I'd reached for it, the screen lighting up with a faint blue glow.

It was late—too late to call. But I hesitated anyway, my thumb hovering over my daughter's name in my contacts. Elle. She was on her own now, old enough to understand the fights, the slammed doors, the silence that had grown thicker than the smoke in these woods. I wondered if she was asleep, if she was safe, if she hated me for not being there full time over her high school years.

The thought twisted in my gut like a knife. I'd done everything I could, but Lydia's take on me as a person was toxic. I had no idea what stories she'd filled Elle's head with.

Ironic, considering the stories I'd wanted to tell but hadn't. I shoved the phone back into my pocket, the weight of it pressing against my thigh.

An hour later— or three? Time bled together on the line— my radio sparked to life again.

"Wind's shifted." Tiff's voice was terse.

I hit the button and held the radio close to my lips. "And?"

"Call the guys back. We're packing up."

I cursed under my breath, then called out the orders on the

line. I pulled out my cell, but didn't bother texting. Tiff was already on it by the twenty-two text message notifications already blinking on my screen.

We moved. Fast. It was what we'd all been trained to do.

And still the evacuation of the camp was a symphony of chaos. We cleared out the equipment, broke down the tent, and started in on the trailers. My mind raced ahead, trying to make sure I wasn't missing anything that would cost my team or the other teams at our side a life.

As the last of the crew piled into the trucks, I turned toward my trailer, only then remembering I wasn't alone. I started running. Mia and Liam were still inside, oblivious to the danger closing in. And I'd locked the damn door.

I burst through the door. "Liam, up! We need to move, now!" I flicked on a light and started closing the straps on the cupboard doors.

Liam shot up, his eyes bleary. "What's going on?"

"The fire's moving fast. We need to get out of here." I left no room for questions. Liam nodded, scrambling to his feet with surprising speed. Maybe I'd misjudged him.

I turned to the curtains that separated my room from the main living area. I didn't want to go in there, but I didn't exactly have a choice. I shouldn't have cared what Mia thought of me, but I didn't relish the thought of adding to her obvious dislike.

I pulled back the curtains, and the words I'd been about to shout died in my throat. Mia lay on the bed, her leg thrown carelessly over the comforter, her body illuminated by the faint light seeping through the blinds. Her pants were draped on the edge of the bed. She was in her shirt and . . . underwear.

I swallowed hard, forcing my eyes from her smooth skin and her dark hair fanning over my pillow. "Mia, wake up!" I barked.

She stirred, her eyes fluttering open in confusion. She sat up with a start, her breath catching as she saw me standing over her. "What—did I—?"

I leaned over, reaching for the keys to my truck on the shelf next to the bed. "The fire's heading straight for us. We need to—"

I didn't finish my sentence. Because something struck me in the face. Hard.

FIVE

MIA

My eyes snapped open, my heart pounding like a wild animal in my chest. Nothing looked familiar, especially the outline of a gargantuan man looming over me. My wolf surged, and I couldn't hear the words coming out of his mouth. Then he moved in, and instinct took over.

My arm shot out, the palm of my hand connecting with his face.

"Shit, Mia!" he stumbled back, but couldn't go very far. He smashed into the cabinets at the foot of the bed and fell forward, bracing himself on the mattress with one hand while still holding his nose.

Connor. I was in his trailer. We'd been waiting for him to fall asleep and—

Air slipped over my skin, and my eyes dropped. What the hell? I wasn't wearing pants? I tried to throw the blanket over myself but it snagged on Connor's arm. "Serves you right! You don't come into someone's bedroom—"

"It's *my* bedroom." Connor groaned then forced himself up as my eyes adjusted. I couldn't make out the features on his face with the backlighting from the living area. He sniffed and held his hand up to the light. No blood. I hadn't hit him that hard, had I?

Connor's eyes dropped, and when he saw my bare legs, he spun fast enough to dry a salad. "The fire's too close. I need to hook up the trailer."

I swung my legs over the side of the bed. Too close? I glanced out the window, but the sky was still pitch black. "What time is it?"

Connor took a few steps, then stopped, planting his hands on his hips. "Doesn't matter. Can you hand me my keys?"

I glanced down, spotting them on the shelf next to the bed. Ah. That's what he was reaching for. I picked them up and held them out. Connor didn't look at me as he took them from my outstretched hand. I was glad he didn't expect an apology because I wasn't going to give him one.

He stalked toward the front of the truck. I closed the curtains, and my hands trembled as I pulled on my pants and grabbed my pack. There wasn't a clock in the room, so I pulled out my phone. Three in the morning. Fantastic.

Should we make a run for it? Liam's voice filtered into my groggy thoughts. I put on my boots and stepped out into the living area. Connor was nowhere to be found.

He's out there? I asked, not willing to say anything out loud just in case.

The door banged open. "A little help?"

Liam gave me a questioning look. I grimaced, then nodded. I'd just impacted the man's nose into his skull. The least we could do is help him with the trailer.

Liam and I stepped outside and threw our packs on the dry grass and gaped. The place was empty. No fire trucks, no tent. There was one other trailer backing out, but otherwise the clearing was empty.

"That was fast," I murmured.

"Tie that down," he jerked his head toward the canopy on the trailer.

Liam moved, but I shook my head and grabbed the rope looped around the hook by the door. "I've got it. Any special instructions?"

"Tight."

Excellent. I would've flipped Connor off had his nose not looked like an oversized strawberry.

Connor got into his truck as Liam gripped the jack handle, working to crank the trailer up just enough for Connor to back the truck into place. The metal groaned as it lifted, the worn wooden blocks underneath shifting slightly before Liam kicked them aside.

"Hold," Liam called out. Connor gave a quick nod, his arm hanging out the window, before easing the truck into reverse, his movements smooth, controlled—not hesitant or trial and error. The hitch lined up perfectly with the coupler on the first try.

I folded my arms, shifting my weight as my wolf perked up again. She'd been prowling since the heel of the hand to the face incident, but now she was intent. Curious. The Connor I'd known ten years ago hadn't been this rough around the edges. He'd been business casual. Clean cut. Charming in that easy, too-smooth kind of way.

But not this. Back then, I couldn't have imagined him in work boots and a faded flannel, sleeves rolled up to forearms lined with muscle, like he actually used them for something other than texting or ordering take out. What had happened to them? I wasn't going to ask.

"Drop it," Connor called, cutting the engine and stepping out.

Liam released the jack, lowering the trailer onto the hitch with a solid clunk. Connor immediately bent to secure it, checking the lock, then giving it a firm shake to make sure it was set.

I hovered, feeling useless. Connor straightened, wiping his hands on his jeans, then flicked his gaze to mine. "Get in." His voice was all business.

I hesitated for half a second too long, but the wind picked up, carrying the scent of smoke.

Mia, we have no idea where this fire is going. It's not safe. Liam shot me a look.

We can shift—

Wolves die just as fast as humans in wildfires. Liam's eyes bore into me.

Right. My heart picked up speed. "My sister—"

"There's nothing you can do right now," Connor barked. "Get in the truck. Please."

The last thing I wanted to do was follow his orders, but then I remembered his hands around my waist. Part of me wanted to be a brat just to see if he'd do it again.

But there wasn't time to question things. Liam and I weren't going to know which way to go even if we did shift and make a break for it. He seemed to be thinking the same thing as he stood and turned to face me.

So. I climbed into the truck.

Connor started the engine, the rumble loud as we pulled away. The world outside was a nightmare—trees shrouded in smoke, the sky a sickly orange haze. Ash fell like rain, landing on the windshield with a soft patter.

I sat rigid in the middle, Connor on my left, Liam on my right. I would've gladly taken shotgun, but I was the smallest of the two of them and Connor's backseat was filled with equipment.

I pressed my hand against my knee to keep it from bouncing, pressure building behind my eyes. *Where was she?* My wolf let out a low whine. Somehow, in my head, it made sense that we were just going to come up here, hunt around until we caught her scent, and talk some sense into her. But this?

I stared out the window at the wall of thick black smoke to the north.

I get that he's not your favorite person, but this is insane, Liam said through our pack bond.

Yeah. I thought back to the grass fire in Kitimat. How the firefighters had strapped on their gear and run straight into the flames.

"Thank you," Liam said. I blinked.

Connor's hands slid an inch on the wheel. "We're not out of the woods yet."

Liam nodded. "No, I meant thank you to you and your team for doing this. Fighting the fire. I see stuff like this on the news but don't think about the people here. Boots on the ground."

My voice caught in my throat. That was exactly like Liam. He didn't have a vengeful bone in his body. I swallowed hard. How much had I taken for granted in my life? Men and women fighting battles like this every day so I could sit comfortable in my living room?

Connor pressed his foot on the gas as we passed the barricade. His thigh rubbed against mine, and my heart jolted. "It's my job."

Liam raised an eyebrow. "Yeah. But you could quit."

A muscle in his jaw tensed. "Not an option for me."

I wasn't sure what he meant by that, but all thoughts slipped from my mind as I glanced down and saw Connor's left hand. No ring. No tan line where a ring might've been. My curiosity grew by the second.

Okay. We can go back to hating him now. Liam sent into my thoughts, keeping his eyes trained out the window.

I somehow kept myself from snorting. *Perfect. Thanks for permission.*

What next, oh wise one?

I didn't know what came next, and I definitely didn't feel wise. The opposite, actually. We had to stay safe. But if the fire was shifting, where would Erin have gone? Further north? Would she have listened to any evacuation orders? Doubtful. If I knew my sister, she was probably sheltering people in an underground bunker or something.

I bit the inside of my cheek. Who was I to think I could come up here and find anyone? Why hadn't I done it sooner? Before Erin was in physical danger?

Here I was focusing on how I couldn't stand Connor Bastien when I should've been troubleshooting. I fought the lump in my throat. I couldn't save my mom, so why did I think I could save my sister?

When we're safe, we'll find a way back to Kitimat, I sent to Liam. *This was a stupid idea.* I didn't want to quit. But what other options did we have? We were in way over our heads.

Liam patted my knee. Connor dropped his eyes, then tightened his grip on the wheel. We drove as fast as the truck would go dragging the trailer and eventually caught up to other emergency vehicles—trailers, fire trucks, and civilian vehicles. We were not alone in this desperate exodus.

Connor ran a hand over stubble on his jaw. "You couldn't text your sister?" He didn't take his eyes off the road.

I tensed, my fingers knotting in my lap. "No."

"Why not?"

The question made my ribs knit. "It's complicated," I snapped. "How's Elle?"

He glanced over at me then turned back to the road. "It's complicated," Connor parroted, his voice flat.

I didn't respond, hoping he'd see the irony in the situation. He could dish it out but couldn't take it. Connor didn't say anything else. The truck rumbled on. I tried not to be distracted by Connor's leg jostling next to mine or the way I could still catch his smell beneath the smoke and dirt. I allowed the hum of the engine to lull me and tried not to jump at the occasional crackle of the radio.

As we drove further south, then east into the rugged backlands, the terrain grew rougher, the road winding through dense forests and rocky outcroppings.

Connor finally spoke as we followed a fire truck down an unkempt lane through the trees. "We're heading for a staging area about twenty kilometers east of here. It's one of the few safe zones left. There will be townsfolk there. We'll find you a ride home."

I turned to him, my throat dry. "And if the fire shifts again?"

Connor's expression was grim. "We'll cross that bridge when we come to it."

I nodded, but the words did little to ease the knot of fear in my chest. Our caravan wound its way through the backlands then finally slowed, the vehicles bunching together as we approached the safe zone. Outlines of cabins sat in the distance.

"I had no idea people lived out here," I murmured.

"Out in the sticks. Isn't that the dream?" Connor dropped his hands from the wheel.

I folded my arms tighter over myself. For some people. Others just wanted their sisters to come home for Christmas dinner.

"Is that a Colorado license plate?" Liam tilted his head, peering through the windshield.

Connor nodded. "They've had to call in help from other provinces and the States. It's a logistical nightmare." He exhaled, tapping a finger on his knee. "Resources are stretched thin. We've got hotshot crews from Alberta, tankers from the U.S., but it's never enough. The fire's been too unpredictable."

Liam leaned forward. "And the origin? They still think it was a lightning strike?"

Connor's jaw clenched. "That's the official line, but I've never seen a fire like this. The way it spreads, the wind shift . . . it's like it has a mind of its own."

I frowned, a shiver running down my spine. "What do you mean?"

"The winds are shifting in patterns I've never seen. One minute it's blowing east, the next west. It's not following the predictive models."

We started inching forward and eventually peeled off to park in a clearing much like the last one we left, but this one was surrounded by homes.

Connor pulled the truck to a stop, but before he could open the door, something caught my eye—a figure standing at the edge of the clearing, her arms crossed.

My heart skipped a beat as recognition hit me like a punch to the gut. It was Lana, her sharp features unmistakable even through the haze. I gasped. Rowan hadn't said much about her absence, but none of us had seen her in weeks.

Connor's gaze snapped to mine in the rearview mirror. "What is it?"

But I couldn't answer. My eyes were locked on Lana as she lifted her gaze to meet mine. Her voice snapped inside my head.

Mia? What the hell are you doing here?

Connor

Mia shoved Liam out of the passenger door and bolted toward a woman across the clearing from where I'd parked the truck. She had dark hair pulled back into a braid, and she rushed forward before Mia could break into a jog. I got out, the soles of my boots sinking into the soft earth. The grass was green here, probably because we were in the valley.

I walked forward with Liam, and as we drew closer, I realized I'd seen that woman a handful of times before in Kitimat, always flanked by Rowan and some other hyper masculine friend who looked like their joint bodyguard. But it was Rowan who'd always drawn my attention. He was so involved in the community, and I couldn't figure out why. He was young and had a lot going for him, and yet he chose to live on the edge of town and work at an auto shop?

Mia threw her arms around the woman, and something about all of this didn't sit right. I'd learned to trust my instincts over the years, and they were screaming at me to be wary. I glanced around, taking in the scattering of locals, their faces set in hard lines. None of them looked happy to see us.

Before I could process much more, a figure emerged from the crowd, his broad frame and rough demeanor making him impossible to ignore. His face was a map of hard lines, his eyes glinting with what I could only assume was red hot rage based on his clenched fists. Where did they pick these men up? Did they recruit them from MMA?

"He looks friendly." A voice sounded next to me, and I frowned. Liam planted himself at my side.

I didn't have time to parse out that interaction. The incoming Momoa stopped a few feet away from me, his fists clenched at his sides. "You shouldn't be here." His gaze flicked to the team of firefighters unloading gear behind me. "This is our land. We don't need your help."

I met his stare head-on, my own jaw clenching. "You need our help," I said, my voice firm but even. "You need it bad." I gestured to the wall of smoke creeping closer, the orange glow of the fire's edge flickering like hell's own light. "That's moving fast. If we don't get ahead of it, it'll burn everything in its path."

The man snorted, a harsh, guttural sound. "You think you can just waltz in here and take over? This is our forest. We know it better than a city boy ever could."

I held up my hands, ignoring that dig. Maybe I'd been a preppy city boy once, but I sure as hell wasn't now. "I'm not here to take over. I'm here to make sure no one dies." I took a step forward, my eyes locked on his. "You think you can handle this on your own? Look at the size of that beast. You can't contain that with local efforts alone. We've got firefighters, aircraft support, equipment—"

"We don't need your equipment!" he barked. "We've been handling fires up here for decades without your help. You think you can just come in and fix everything with your fancy gear, but you don't know the first thing about this land."

And here we go. I exhaled, crossing my arms over my chest. These northerners couldn't have been more pretentious if they tried.

"Then why isn't it handled?" Liam cocked his head to the side.

"Who is this, your lap dog?"

I shook my head. "He's not with me."

Liam waved me off. "Oh, I'm with him. I slept in his bed last night—"

"Can you shut the hell up?" I was point five seconds away from giving him a matching swollen nose. My mind scrambled for something solid. This fire was spreading at seventy meters per minute, fueled by winds that were gusting unpredictably. The containment efforts were at a dismal twenty-three percent, and the evacuation alerts had already displaced hundreds. This wasn't just about pride or territory. This was about survival.

"This isn't about who knows the land better," I said finally, my voice hard. If it was, I definitely would've won, but I kept that to myself. "It's about stopping that fire before it's too late. We're losing ground. Fast. If we don't cut it off now, it'll keep spreading, and there won't be anyone left to protect."

Our argument was drawing attention. Handfuls of locals and emergency personnel crowded in closer. Perfect. I'd entered a pissing match without my knowledge. I took a step forward. "Listen. I get that you don't want us touching your trees. But if we don't take down a perimeter, we'll lose all of them. We use my strategy, we barely lose an extra five percent."

Before he could respond, the woman with the braid stepped forward with Mia, stopping next to his side.

Mia positioned herself between them. "Connor, meet Lana. A friend from Kitimat."

Lana put out a hand, and I shook it. "This is my m—partner. Destin." She took the hand of the man who had been seconds away from cussing me out, and his face visibly softened.

Interesting. "Nice to meet you." I held out my hand to Destin, but he didn't take it initially. Then with a glower, he shook.

"I'm Liam." He held out his hand and Destin looked at it like Liam had just smeared it in dog shit.

Lana laughed. "He's a friend. They both are." She glanced up at me. "And I know him from Kitimat."

Destin ground his teeth, but snapped his mouth closed.

Lana fixed her eyes on me. "You might be fire chief back home, but you don't mess with the people here. They're our responsibility, and I don't want anyone questioning them."

I nodded once. "Fine."

"And we want access to your data. Maps, predictive models, everything," she added.

"I can do that." She could look at the maps if she wanted. They weren't going to mean anything to her.

Lana looked up at Destin. He drew a breath, then exhaled slowly. He jerked a thumb toward the edge of the clearing. "You can park your gear over there. But if you so much as scratch one tree without our say-so, you're out."

I nodded, a curt, sharp movement. "Understood."

Once I gave the word, our firefighters moved quickly. The trailers rumbled into place, and the tent popped up before I finished unhooking mine from the hitch. After we were somewhat settled, I sought out Destin again.

Liam and Mia had disappeared somewhere, but now that they had a friend, I figured I was off the hook. I frowned, wondering why that made my stomach sink.

Destin jumped in with us, working on the line and bringing in a few other men and women to assist. My muscles burned by the time the sun set, the sky painted in hues of vibrant orange and red. The one gift from the smoke hovering in the atmosphere.

I needed a shower. I needed—

I froze as I turned to swing my axe again. Mia. She was walking away from someone, her head bowed.

Irritation surged through me. What was she doing? She should be back at the cabins, safe. I adjusted my hard hat and reached for the chainsaw that sat at my feet, but before I could pull the cord, I set it back down again. It was about time for my break. And I needed fresh water anyway.

CHAPTER
SEVEN

MIA

The world around me blurred as I pressed my back against the rough exterior of the log cabin. *Last I heard, she was near Nass Camp.*

My sister.

Destin had knowledge that she was in the path of destruction.

I was an idiot for not working harder to get in touch with her. Some twisted part of me believed that she was the one who should make the effort. She was the older sister. But now, I berated myself for not swallowing my pride and hitching a ride north sooner.

I couldn't lose her. There were too many questions I had for her, too many words I needed to say.

"Mia!" Destin's voice cut through the fog of my thoughts. I turned my face, not wanting him to see my tear streaked cheeks as he rounded the back of the house still in his fire gear. His footsteps slowed. "Mia, I didn't mean—"

"Destin, what the hell?" Lana muttered. She stopped next to me, her hand on my shoulder, warm and steady. "Mia, breathe. Just breathe."

I wanted to push her away, to tell her I was fine, but the words caught in my throat. My mind raced, a relentless cycle of fear. Erin. *Erin. Erin.* Her name echoed in my head, a mantra of dread. I'd said her name, and Destin's face had changed, a flicker passing through his expression. I couldn't let it go without knowing.

"We don't know anything yet," Destin grunted. "She's a rogue. Cares about her community and has stepped in to help on more than one occasion. They were given evacuation orders just like everyone else."

"But did she follow them?" I demanded, my voice breaking. Of course Erin cared. She'd had a bleeding heart since she was a toddler. That's exactly why I was worried about her. I swiped at my cheeks and turned to face them. "Can you feel her? Through pack bonds?"

"Rogues don't have packs," Lana explained, her voice softer. "They don't have bonds."

Destin nodded. "We don't balk at connection, but most give up their bonds. I can't reach them, Mia. I can't tell you anything more."

I exhaled, my hands trembling. Give them up. Would Erin have really gone that far? I'd always assumed it was distance that made it impossible to feel her or talk with her. But what if it was more than that?

I pressed my palms against the rough bark of the logs behind me, inhaling the fresh scent of pine.

Lana's hand tightened on my shoulder, a steady presence. "We don't know the full extent of the fire yet." Her voice was calm, a balm to the raw edges of my panic. "The north has safe zones. Most people likely escaped."

I turned to her, my eyes searching hers. She believed what she was saying. "What are you doing here, Lana?"

Her lips parted in surprise at the question. Was it really that shocking that I'd ask? She'd been gone from Kitimat for weeks. At least when Jasper left, we got some kind of report. With Lana? Rowan hadn't said a word. And now here she was with this man who seemed like her fated mate.

"Mia—"

The sound of boots crunching on gravel silenced us all. Connor appeared around the corner, his broad frame filling the space. He scanned the scene, his gaze lingering on each of us before settling on me. "What's going on?"

I opened my mouth to speak, but nothing came out. Lana stepped in, her voice smooth. "Nothing, Connor. Just a misunderstanding."

But Connor's eyes didn't leave mine. There was no point in pretending I wasn't emotionally compromised. My eyes felt like they'd been rubbed with cat hair.

Connor shoved a hand in the pocket of his jeans. "We're preparing a line. If you have information—"

"They don't." I could see where his head was going. Us having a secret meeting behind the house. And I knew he wasn't one to give up easily if he still had questions. "This is a personal matter."

Connor assessed the three of us. "I expect to be looped in. If I'm giving you information—"

"You haven't given us shit." Destin positioned himself between Connor and the two of us. "Any looping will be on my timeline."

I pushed off the logs and stepped forward. "Just loop, okay? We need to stop this fire. You're both on the same team." My fear and grief eclipsed my personal vendetta against Connor at the moment. If we didn't work together, we were never going to get this thing under control.

Connor's jaw tightened, his eyes narrowing as he bit his tongue. For a moment, I thought he would walk away, but then he spoke, his voice gruff. "Satellite images show small safe pockets up north." He ran a hand through his hair. "If you're wondering about the people up there."

People? I'd told Connor I was looking for my sister, but had I mentioned where I thought she was? Was he offering this information as . . . a kindness?

"Normally I would have a sense of evacuation numbers," he continued, "but this fire's spread is unpredictable, shifting winds . . . it's like nothing I've seen before. Communication's have been knocked out. I don't think we'll know much more until containment increases."

Destin's head snapped up, his rough features sharpening with interest. "What are you talking about?"

Lana's back straightened. Her eyes flicked to Destin, and I knew that look. They were communicating about something.

"The wind?" Connor shrugged. "The models can't quantify it. There's some strange updraft—"

"Let me see it." Destin was already stalking forward.

My eyes narrowed as Lana followed, brushing past Connor. *What did they know?* She was hiding something, and so was Destin. Did they know something about the fire? Or was there something else going on that I wasn't privy to? Something even Rowan wasn't talking about at home?

"Asshole," Connor muttered, then turned and followed Lana and Destin.

I jogged after them, not waiting to be invited. If they knew something, I was going to be in that room when they dropped a clue.

EIGHT

The tent was barely functional by the time I leaned over the central console, my fingers tracing the glowing lines of wind patterns on the screen. Lana and Momoa stood on either side of me. Not anxiety inducing in the least.

Especially considering the data. The fire was spreading faster than we'd anticipated, and the wind patterns were shifting in ways that defied logic. "See this?" I jabbed at a swirling mass of color on the screen. "This isn't just a typical wind shift. It's rotating."

"Like a tornado," Lana murmured.

I grunted. "More like a hurricane."

She crossed her arms, her dark braid falling over her shoulder as she tilted her head. "A hurricane? You're telling me the fire is acting like a hurricane?"

"Not exactly." My mind raced, analyzing the new satellite images. "But the principles are the same. The heat from the fire is creating a low-pressure system, drawing in the surrounding air. If the winds keep rotating like this, it could develop into something self-sustaining. I've studied firestorms before, but this is different."

Destin's expression was hard. "Deliberate?"

I frowned. Even if someone started the fire, how could they control something like this? "I didn't say that. I said it's unusual. Fires don't naturally form rotation like this. It's too symmetrical, too controlled. I don't understand how this could be caused by wind patterns—it's a system. A damned perfect one."

My thoughts drifted back to my training days, the endless hours of studying burn patterns and wind dynamics. My instructor, a grizzled old firefighter named Mack, used to drill into us the importance of reading the signs. "Fire doesn't lie," he'd say. "It tells you everything you need to know if you're willing to listen." I'd always been good at listening, at picking up on the subtle cues that others missed. It's what made me a decent fire chief.

I wondered what Mack would've said about this. I'd spent years honing my instincts, learning to trust the little voice in the back of my head that screamed when something was off. And right now, that voice was deafening.

Lana and Destin exchanged a look. "We'll get our people ready," Lana said finally, her voice crisp. "If this thing is going to blow south, we need to be prepared."

I nodded, but my eyes stayed glued to the screen. "I want everyone ready to move at a moment's notice. If this fire starts moving like I think it will, we'll need every option available."

Destin grunted again, his massive frame shifting as he turned for the door. "On it."

Mia still stood in the corner, her eyes dark and shrewd. But it wasn't me that she was observing. It was her two friends. She turned to me once, then quickly looked away. It's not like we were besties, as my daughter would say, but I didn't expect the silent treatment. Had waking her up that morning pissed her off that bad?

I had to stop thinking about waking her up. That image of her long, silky legs was burned in my brain, and it wasn't helping me focus. All three of them left, the trailer's metal door clanging shut behind them. The sudden silence was a relief.

I sank back into the creaky office chair, my elbows resting on my knees as I stared at the screen. The rotating mass of wind and fire seemed to pulse, like a living thing. My mind raced, pulling up every case study, every disaster, every freak occurrence I'd ever heard of. Nothing fit.

The trailer's heater kicked on, spewing a stream of warm air that carried the faint scent of diesel. I rubbed my eyes, the grit of lack of sleep scratching at my lids. I needed to focus. I needed answers.

But the more I stared at the data, the more questions I had. Where was this rotation coming from? Why was it so perfect? *Deliberate? The* idea was ludicrous.

I pushed to my feet, my joints cracking in protest. The trailer was small, and I paced its length, trying to burn off the restless energy coiling in my gut.

I needed to move.

I shoved my feet back into my boots and left the trailer, walking to the command tent. The air was brisk now that we were further from the blaze.

I stepped inside the tent, the heavy canvas flap swinging shut behind me. The team was gathered around the central table, their faces lit by the harsh glare of construction lights.

Tiff looked up, her eyes wide. "Connor," Tiff straightened, her voice a little too bright, a little too quick. "Just getting updated on the fire lines."

The others—Jesse, Marco, and Elena—stood at attention, and I froze. "What the hell is going on?" My gut tightened as I waited for the worst. I didn't know how much more bad news I could take.

"Nothing." Marco shoved his hands in his pockets.

"Uh-huh." My eyes narrowed.

"Yeah," Jesse said, too fast, his eyes darting to Tiff before settling on me. "Just . . . you know, the usual chaos."

I crossed my arms, leaning against the metal frame of the tent. "The usual chaos doesn't make you all look like you've shit your pants."

Marco shifted, his broad shoulders rolling in a shrug. "Nothing, man. Just . . . uh . . . some rumors about evacuations."

I narrowed my eyes. "Rumors? From who?"

Elena fidgeted with the hem of her jacket. "Just . . . stuff floating around. Doesn't matter."

"Doesn't matter?" I straightened, my voice hardening. "If it's about this crisis, it damn well matters. Spit it out."

Tiff sighed, her hands planting on her hips. "Connor, it's not about evacuations. It's personal."

The word hit me like a punch to the gut. Personal. Tiff rarely got personal. Which meant that whatever it was, it was about me. And from the way they were acting, it wasn't good.

"What is it?" I demanded, my patience fraying.

Marco hesitated, then lifted his phone, the screen glowing with a social media page. I didn't need to see the image to know I wasn't going to like it. The way Marco's face tightened, the way Elena looked away—whatever it was, it was bad.

"Show me," I said, my voice steady, though my blood was pounding in my ears.

He handed me the phone. And there it was. A picture of my ex-wife, smiling, her arms wrapped around another man. Not just any man—the twenty-five-year-old from her office who she had an affair with. The caption underneath was somehow worse.

LIVING *my best life with my soulmate. #blessed #happilyeverafter.*

A RAZOR BLADE wedged between my ribs. For a moment, I couldn't breathe, couldn't think. The room around me faded, and I was back to the day I found out she'd cheated on me. The day my world shattered.

It had been a crisp autumn afternoon. I'd been at the fire station, exhausted from a long call the night before. And then Jake, one of the younger guys on the team, had pulled me aside. His face had been pale, his eyes avoiding mine as he awkwardly relayed how he'd seen my wife checking into a hotel with a guy he knew from his tennis club.

I'd laughed. I'd actually laughed, because it was so absurd. My wife—my partner, my best friend—would never do that. She loved me. I knew she did. But Jake's expression had stopped me cold. He wasn't lying.

It all blew up the night she wore that red dress.

The next week, I went home, my heart in my throat, and found her in our bedroom. She was packing, her suitcase open on the bed, clothes scattered around her. And she'd looked up at me, her eyes hard, her face cold.

"You're suffocating me," she'd said, her voice flat. "You're never here, Connor. You're always at the firehouse, always putting your job first. I need someone who actually wants to be with me."

I stood there, frozen, as she told me she was leaving. As she told me she'd been seeing someone else for months. As she told me I was the problem.

And then she'd walked out. Just like that.

The memory slammed into me like a freight train, leaving me breathless. I blinked, forcing myself back to the present. The command tent. The phone still clutched in my hand. The team watching me, their faces a mix of pity and discomfort.

I handed the phone back to Marco. "So," I kept my voice even, though my insides were raw. "She's moved on. Good for her."

But the words felt like ash in my mouth. Frustration burned in my chest, the disbelief clawing at my throat. She'd done it again. She'd hurt me again. And I said I'd never let that happen.

"Connor," Tiff said softly, her hand reaching out.

I shook my head, stepping back. "I'm fine," I lied. "It's old wounds, that's all."

But it wasn't fine. It wasn't old. It was fresh, raw, gaping. And I couldn't let them see that. I couldn't let them know how much it still hurt.

I turned, heading for the tent flap. "I need some air," I said, my voice rough.

"Connor—" Tiff started.

But I was already gone, stepping out into the cold, the ash-filled air stinging my eyes. I didn't know where I was going. I just knew I had to get out. Had to clear my head. Had to remind myself that this—this pain, this betrayal—it wasn't mine to carry anymore. Much easier said than done.

I started walking, my boots crunching over the uneven ground. And then as I wove past a trailer, I slammed into something—someone.

"Oh!" she exclaimed as I gasped. I stumbled back as a hot liquid soaked through my shirt.

MIA

"I'm so sorry!" The words spilled out of me as I stared in horror at the soup stain spreading across Connor's shirt. My wolf stood at attention as I clutched the now-empty bowl. *It's fine, girl. I'm just a clutz.* "I didn't see you there, I was just—"

Connor grimaced, plucking at the soaked fabric. "It's fine," he grumbled, but his tight jaw betrayed his annoyance.

"No, please, let me help clean it up," I insisted, setting the bowl down on the ground and pulling off my cardigan. My face burned with embarrassment as I dabbed at the stain ineffectually. How had I not seen him coming around the corner?

The whole thing was a stupid idea. There was no reason for me to bring him food in the first place, but I was sick of being pissed off every time I looked at him. I didn't have to like him to respect that he was trying to do his best protecting lives. I thought offering an olive branch would help convince my stomach to stop twisting every time I saw him.

Not that it would matter much after tonight.

Connor's large hand closed over mine, stilling my frantic motions. "I said it's fine, Mia. I'll take care of it."

My wolf lit up from the inside out. She pressed forward, leaning into his touch. She let out a low whine as he turned abruptly and strode off toward his trailer, leaving me standing there with a damp sweater.

What the—

My wolf lunged, propelling me forward. My mind reeled as I hurried after him. *It wasn't fully my fault!* I hissed, but that did nothing to stop her from breathing down my neck. *Fine. I get it. I need to make this right.*

I caught up to him just as he reached his trailer door. "Connor, wait," I called out breathlessly. "Do you even have a washing machine?"

He paused, one hand on the door handle, and looked back at me. His hazel eyes were unreadable. "I have a sink."

I frowned. "Gross."

The corner of his mouth twitched. "Thanks for that." He pulled the door open, but I put out a hand.

"There's a washer and dryer in the cabin. And a nice shower."

Connor studied me for a long moment. "Who was the stew for."

My heart kicked up a notch. "There was extra."

"It was for me?"

I nodded once, not able to maintain eye contact. I flinched as Connor reached out and took the soiled bowl from my hands. He lifted the dirty spoon and scooped what was left of the stew into his mouth.

I held my breath, stunned as he looked up at me past hooded brows. Heat flared in my middle. What the hell was this? The discomfort bubbled up and boiled over, which for me looked like a shit ton of blabber. "I haven't seen you eat since last night and even though I didn't want to stay in your trailer, you kept us safe. So this is me saying thank you. I think we're even now."

Connor chewed, his expression unreadable. "Even." He handed the bowl back to me.

"Well, after I get your shirt clean. And you. I mean, you should shower—not should, but could if you wanted a better shower than the one here—"

Connor opened the door and stepped inside the trailer. It swung closed with a clang. Damn it. What was that all about? We're even? I hadn't been keeping score, and if I had been, we weren't even close. He cost my mother her love of life, there wasn't anything he could do to repay that.

My wolf pressed. *And yet . . .*

He still didn't have a way to wash that shirt.

I tapped my foot on the ground and growled as I pulled the door open and tromped up after him. "Connor—"

He looked up, his flannel wadded in his hands. My breath caught in my throat at the sight of his bare skin, the play of muscles beneath the surface. It was obvious that Connor was fit, but seeing him like that sent a jolt through me.

Realizing I was staring, I quickly averted my gaze, a flush creeping up my neck. "I, um . . . I'll just—"

"There's stain remover under the sink." He set the shirt on the strip of kitchen counter in front of him.

I nodded, transfixed, as he stalked toward his bedroom. "You're going to insist we do this in the sink?"

"Do what?" Connor glanced over his shoulder, and a blush hit my cheeks fast enough to make me heady.

"Clean the stain," I snapped. "There's a washer and dryer—"

"Appreciate the offer, but it's not necessary," he called from behind the curtain. "I can handle it myself."

I set my jaw. "You're not handling it. I'm handling it, and I'm going to take it up to the house. In fact, why don't you get the rest of your dirty clothes and I'll take them up, too."

He stepped back into the living area, pulling a clean T-shirt over his torso, the fabric stretching across his shoulders. We stared at each other for a long moment. "My laundry will smell like smoke in point five seconds after they're washed."

"Better than sweat and smoke."

He raised an eyebrow. "Would you like to give a formal complaint?"

"I don't give a shit either way, but I think—"

"You seem to give plenty of shits."

I snapped my mouth closed. "I'm trying to be nice."

"Why?"

The question reverberated through me. Because I feel helpless. Because I don't know if my sister is alive and that makes everything else matter less. Because I'm sick of carrying anger in my heart.

Tears pricked the corners of my eyes, but I pushed them back, clenching my jaw. "I don't need a reason to be kind."

Connor drew a breath. Then he turned and stepped back into his bedroom. When the curtain swung open again, Connor was holding a small pile of laundry and a folded pair of ... boxer briefs.

Hmm. Black.

We walked across the clearing, and the warm glow of the cabin enveloped us as Destin's friend, Sue, opened the door with a welcoming smile. "Did he like the—Oh!" Her eyes sparkled with kindness and a hint of mischief as she looked up at Connor and took the empty bowl from my hands.

"I wondered if Connor could use the washer."

Sue smiled and moved back so we could enter. "Of course, of course. No trouble at all, honey. Any friend of Destin's is a friend of mine."

"I'm not exactly a friend." Connor shifted on his feet.

Sue winked. "Even better."

We took off our shoes and Sue led Connor toward the laundry room. I trailed behind, my heart pounding in my chest as we passed another shifter in the hall. Didn't think about that when I let him follow me to the cabin instead of handing over his clothes. This cabin was full of shifters. The last thing any of us needed was the fire chief observing us.

Sue insisted on taking the clothes, then asked twenty questions about the stain on his shirt. She agreed that a shower was absolutely necessary and shooed him into the bedroom off the hall.

I retreated, leaving her to it. When she reappeared in the hall and closed the door behind her, I finally drew a full breath. He was contained. Showering.

"I'll put this on a quick wash. This machine is built with the same parts as a jet engine, did you know that?" Sue announced as she walked back to the laundry room. I retreated to the living area and sat in an armchair next to the fire.

Well. That was . . . unexpected. My wolf lay comfortably, licking her paws. As if she hadn't just thrown me into Connor's trailer and riddled me with guilt.

I curled my legs up onto the cushion. Liam hadn't returned from helping one of Connor's teams that afternoon. Unless they forced him to leave, I doubt he'd be back until he physically crashed, which for shifters could be well past midnight.

I reached out through our pack bond. *Coming back anytime soon? We're leaving in the morning.*

Well aware, Liam shot back. *Trying to do as much as I can.*

I sighed, then glanced around the room. I wasn't going to go join the fire line, but maybe there was something I could do here. I forced myself up and headed for the kitchen. Rolling up my sleeves, I filled the sink with soapy water and started washing the dishes. When that was finished, I wiped down the table, the countertops, and then swept the floor.

A few shifters came and went, some taking food from the fridge and some adding to the supply there. I had no idea where the closest grocery store was, but they seemed to work as a well-oiled machine.

All of it made me think of Erin. Was this how she lived? Did she have friends? People who looked out for her?

While I was dusting in the living room, the buzzer on the washer went off. I waited a moment, then walked to the laundry room and poked my head in. She wasn't there. Setting the dusting rag on the counter, I opened the washer and pulled out Connor's clothes, transferring them to the dryer. As I threw in the last shirt, a small foil square fluttered to the ground.

I bent to pick it up, my breath catching in my throat as I realized what it was. A condom. Unopened.

I pursed my lips. Definitely sleeping with the deputy.

My wolf let out a low growl, and I jumped. What in the world had gotten into her tonight? I set the condom on top of the dryer, not wanting to throw it away, but also blushing at the idea of Sue finding it there. I'd listen for the buzzer a second time, apparently.

The living room wasn't empty when I returned. Men and women streamed in through the front door, chattering and waving when they saw me. I couldn't bring myself to join in. Instead, I found myself drawn to the small, cozy kitchen.

I filled the kettle and set it on the stove, the simple ritual soothing in its familiarity. As I waited for the water to boil, I leaned against the counter, my gaze drifting out the window to the moonlit forest beyond.

Eventually, the kettle whistled, and I busied myself with preparing a steaming mug of chamomile tea. Cradling the warm ceramic in my hands, I breathed in the herbal steam and slipped out the back door, seeking the quiet sanctuary of the porch. I couldn't go to bed until Connor was out of here, so I might as well—

Out of the corner of my eye, I caught a glimpse of something that made my breath catch in my throat. There, through the window, was Connor. He stood in front of the bathroom mirror, naked from the waist up.

Shaving. He was shaving. The muscles of his back rippled as he lifted the electric razor to his face, his skin golden in the warm light of the lamp.

I knew I should look away, give him his privacy. But I couldn't seem to tear my gaze from the sight of him, my heart pounding in my chest. There was something about the vulnerability of the moment, the intimacy of seeing him like this, that made my pulse race.

As I watched, transfixed, Connor turned slightly, his profile coming into view. The strong line of his jaw, the curve of his shoulder . . . it was like seeing him for the first time. Not as Elle's dad. Not as the asshole fire chief. Just a man.

I forced myself to look away, my cheeks burning with shame and confusion. What was wrong with me?

But even as I scolded myself, I couldn't shake the image of him from my mind, the way his skin had gleamed in the lamplight. It was like a switch had been flipped, a door opened that I couldn't seem to close.

I slumped onto a porch chair, my tea forgotten as I stared

out into the night. The moonlight painted the trees in shades of silver and shadow. I don't know how long I sat like that, but I definitely didn't hear the buzzer on the dryer. Or the door to the porch.

But I jumped when Connor appeared in front of me, holding up the condom package between his thumb and forefinger. "I promise, this was a joke."

TEN

CONNOR

I wrapped the towel tighter around my waist, the fabric surprisingly soft against my skin. I wouldn't have taken anyone who lived in the backwoods for a fan of fabric softener.

I ran a hand over my now smooth jaw line and walked into the bedroom. The bed was a simple affair, a sturdy oak frame with a patchwork quilt that looked hand-sewn. My clothes were laid out neatly at the foot, a gesture that made me wonder who had done it. Mia?

That prompted a low burn in my middle. It was just a pair of jeans, a couple of shirts, and a few pairs of underwear. But the idea of her touching my clothes felt . . . strange.

It was probably Sue. The thought sent a flicker of gratitude through me, quickly overshadowed by the awkwardness of the situation. I reached for my shirt, and that's when I saw it—a condom wrapper, placed conspicuously on top of my clothes. My heart skipped a beat as I stared at it, my mind racing.

What the hell? I picked it up, the wrapper crinkling in my hand. It was unopened, but the fact that it was there at all was enough to make my face heat up. A wave of embarrassment washed over me. Who could have put this here?

And then the memory hit me. I groaned. Tiff. *Damn it, Tiff.*

I could almost hear her laughter, sharp and teasing, as she handed me the condom after that apartment fire in Black Lake. It had been a joke, a stupid, ridiculous joke, and at the time, it had been funny. We'd just pulled a family out of a burning building, and the adrenaline was still pumping through me. Tiff found the condom in her pocket—leftover from heaven knows where since she hadn't been with a man since 1997— and handed it to me with a smirk. "For later, hero." She winked, nodding toward the single mom who was still watching me from the curb with doe eyes. I'd taken it, rolled my eyes, and stuffed it into my pocket, forgetting about it until now.

Had I really not washed those jeans until now? I tossed the wrapper onto the bed. The joke was on Tiff, but that? That was on me.

I dropped the towel and pulled on my boxers, then grabbed my shirt and put it on, my skin prickling. I stepped into my jeans, the denim soft and worn, and zipped them up with a jerk. Mia had been right about one thing. A real shower felt damn good. I'd stayed in too long because I couldn't force myself to leave real water pressure.

The trailer was better than nothing, but I missed my house. Missed waking up in the morning and having a cup of coffee.

I blew out a breath. As if I would ever be the guy who relaxed for a living. The adrenaline rush was too addicting.

I stood, running a hand through my damp hair. This was

better. Now all I needed was a real meal and about a week of sleep. What I got was the faint hum of my phone, buzzing with notifications.

I didn't pick it up. Guaranteed that picture of Lydia was all over my feed, and I didn't need to see more. I knew the drill. The perfect life, the perfect partner, the perfect everything. It was all there, curated and polished, and it made me sick.

I should've blocked her, but when we got divorced, I had some stupid idea of being noble. Now if I did it, I'd only look like a schmuck that was still hung up on her. Which I wasn't.

It was never about her. It was always about how she made me feel about myself. And unfortunately, I wasn't having much success turning that train around.

The cabin was quiet as I left the room. I didn't realize I'd been looking for Mia until I entered the living room and found it empty. I wasn't disappointed. It was just strange to be in some stranger's house.

I walked toward the front door, but when I turned to put on my boots, I glanced up and stilled. Mia was sitting outside the window, her back to me. Her legs were curled up, her head tilted back, staring at the sky.

I stood there for a long moment, the internal debate raging. But in the end, it wasn't much of a fight. I grabbed my boots, shoving my feet into them with a practiced ease, and headed for the door.

The porch creaked under my boots as I stepped out into the crisp evening air. The sky was a deep shade of indigo, with stars beginning to peek through the canopy above. How long had it been since I'd seen that?

I hadn't planned to lead with condom banter, but that's what came out of my mouth. "I promise, this was a joke."

Mia blinked, her head turning to me. She glanced at the condom, then back to my face. "Like, a joke for me or for you?"

I breathed a laugh. "Depends. Did you think it was funny?"

She gave me a look. "Kind of a weird power move."

I pulled the other porch chair to the side of hers and sat down. "Arrogant fire chief. Remember?"

She exhaled. "Yeah. Totally tracks."

"I always carry one in my pocket. Comes in handy."

"Mmm. I can only imagine. All those damsels in distress."

"Exactly. Their house is burned to the ground, but I'm just that irresistible."

Mia's mouth quirked, then she wrapped her arms around her knees and stared back up at the stars. I found myself wanting to ask her what she was thinking. Why she was sitting out here alone. But I doubted one spilled bowl of soup and a condom had built the kind of rapport we needed for a conversation like that. My chest tightened at the realization I was even considering a conversation like that.

"The stars aren't like this in Kitimat."

I nodded, looking up. "I'm surprised you can even see anything. It's been smoked over for weeks. Must've gotten a lucky draft."

She wet her lips. "If you find people up north, will you ask for her?"

"Your sister?"

"Erin Hunt. Not sure if she'll go by the same last name, honestly."

I considered this. "You're not staying?" I tried to keep my tone neutral.

Mia shook her head. "Weren't you the one saying we should get the hell home? Liam and I are heading back in the morning. There's probably more I can do to help displaced families there."

I let out a puff of air. She wasn't wrong. But that didn't

explain the strange twisting beneath my ribs. "Good. One less pain in my ass."

Mia laughed out loud, looking as surprised as I was at that reaction. She sighed and rested her chin on her knees. "You're different than you were."

I raised an eyebrow. "Not you. You're exactly the same." Another laugh. I was starting to like the sound of that a little too much.

We sat in silence for a long moment, the only sound the distant howl of a wolf. Mia tensed, then stood abruptly. "I should go inside. It's getting late."

I nodded, but I didn't move. I just sat there, my eyes fixed on the spot where she'd been sitting. She hesitated for a moment, then turned and walked back into the cabin, the door creaking shut behind her.

CHAPTER

ELEVEN

MIA

I stuffed the last of my toiletries into my pack, then stepped out onto the porch. The clearing should have been alive with the chorus of birds, but instead it was dead silent, coated in toxic fog. So much for our lucky draft from the night before.

Liam hadn't finished his breakfast yet—Sue had woken up and made him bacon and eggs. She said it was for both of us, but I wasn't fooled.

I strode toward Lana's truck and caught sight of Connor leaning against his trailer. His hair was mussed, his clothes askew. Was that what he'd been wearing the night before?

"Rough night?" I gave an empathetic smile. I hadn't slept well either.

Connor took a sip of his coffee. "Not the worst."

68

I winced when he tipped his chin, and the bruises under his eyes became visible. "I'm sorry about that."

Connor grunted. Not in the mood to talk this morning it seemed. I turned and was about to throw my pack into the truck when the sound of an engine and tires spitting up gravel roared through the clearing.

I peered through the windshield of the vehicle as it approached, and my eyes widened. Callista?

The truck skidded to a stop, dust curling up in thick plumes around the tires. Before the engine even cut, the door flung open.

Kael hit the ground running, a thin, battered book clutched tight in his hand, his face carved with urgency. Callista was right behind him, slamming the door shut with a sharp thud.

"Where's Lana?" Kael demanded.

I blinked. Not a "hi" or "hello." I wondered if he even knew who I was. I'd heard plenty about him—the story of Callista being hunted had made its way through the entire pack—but had never met him face to face. "Um, inside?" I pointed to the cabin.

Callista barely spared me a glance before heading straight for the steps. My stomach coiled. I didn't think, just jogged after them.

It only took Kael a few minutes to gather everyone. Sue gave us the bedroom next to the laundry room to occupy—the same one Connor had been in the night before—and we all found places to sit. The bed, floor, whatever worked. I sat cross-legged on the floor next to Liam next to the armoire. Destin tried to make me take one of the seats, but I was happy where I was.

Kael glanced at the door to the hall. "Who else is staying here?"

Destin shook his head. "They won't hear a thing. Sue already set a ward."

A ward? I'd only known of a handful of shifters who could work that kind of magic. I thought of Sue washing clothes and cooking breakfast. I shouldn't have judged that book by its cover.

Kael turned to me and Liam. "And you want them here?"

Destin glanced at Lana. She worried her lower lip, considering. "I don't know. But it's only a matter of time before Kitimat Pack and many others know exactly what we're searching for."

My frown deepened by the second. Searching for?

Kael nodded once, then held up the book in his hand. He only had one arm, and my eyes were drawn to the asymmetry. Not in a bad way, but a curious one. The lore that swirled around him in our pack was intriguing to say the least. "This was my mother's journal. We went back for it after we . . . parted ways."

So. They would let us be here, but the weren't going to tell us everything.

Kael cleared his throat. "She wrote about an amulet. And . . . what my father used it for. I don't think my abilities are inborn. I think . . . " Kael's throat worked. "I think he gave them to me."

Lana stilled, and Destin stepped a bit closer to her. I looked between the four of them waiting for anyone to expound on what he just said. We'd rushed into this room to talk about a necklace? And what abilities did Kael have?

Lana blew out a breath, then turned to me and Liam. "Mia, why did you decide to come here?"

My heart picked up speed. "I wanted to find my sister. Make sure she was safe."

Lana nodded. "It felt urgent. Like a call."

My hands began to tingle. I nodded. That was exactly how it felt.

Lana dropped to the bed, bracing herself on her knees. "There's too much evidence. They have to be using it, but I can't see a damn thing—"

Destin dropped a hand on her shoulder as her voice broke. "There must be a reason for it."

I was lost. Completely. Too much evidence of what? I pressed my hands against my knees. "Can someone please explain what is happening right now?"

Callista brushed her hair over her shoulder. "You've heard of the relics."

I scanned my memory. Yes. I'd heard of them. Old fables. "The story of Seraphina?"

Kael looked impressed. "She knows more than you did."

Callista rolled her eyes. "Well, turns out, they exist. Not just in stories."

Lana pulled a dagger from her hip. "This is one. And . . . " She pushed herself up from the bed. Destin looked hesitant to let her go, but she patted his hand. "I'll be right back."

Lana walked out the door, and the room fell into an uncomfortable silence. Then, just as abruptly as she'd left, she was back. The door swung open, and she stepped inside, clutching a book much thicker than Kael's. The cover was black leather, worn and cracked with age, and it seemed to absorb the light around it. She held it like it was a fragile egg, her fingers curled protectively around it.

My wolf stood at attention, her eyes locked on the tome.

"This is The Book of Shadows." Lana placed it on the bed. "It's another relic we paid the price to find. It's the key to finding the amulet, goblet, and crown and understanding the magic. But let me make one thing clear: this isn't something to take lightly. The magic in here . . . " She paused, her dark eyes scanning the room. "It's not just powerful. It's dangerous. And it's not something we can talk about outside these walls. Ever."

The gravity of her words settled over the room. The Book of Shadows seemed to hum with an energy all its own, like it was alive, watching us. My skin itched. I didn't like it. Not one bit.

Lana opened the book, the pages crackling with age. She flipped through them, her fingers careful.

"You can read it?" Kael asked, his voice awed.

Lana nodded, then began to read. "The amulet isn't a trinket. It's a cloak of shadows. It can make the wearer untouchable, untraceable. You could walk through a crowded room and no one would even know you're there."

She turned a page, the parchment-like paper revealing intricate drawings of symbols that made no sense to me. "But this power comes at a high cost. The amulet bonds its wielders, slowly eating away at their souls. Their bodies. It gives wind and shadow, but in return, you are destined to become such."

Something inside my head clicked. Wind. "The fire," I murmured. Connor talked about the drafts, the wind patterns. They were unnatural. Unpredictable. Too perfect.

Lana closed the book and straightened. "Exactly. The fire. There is another realm. Layered over this one. I have searched—"

"Another realm?" Liam's eyes were wide. "What the hell do you mean another realm?"

Destin crossed his arms over his chest. "Can I say it?"

Lana pursed her lips. "Destin—"

"You're talking to the alpha of Shadow Pack. Show some damn respect."

Liam's mouth snapped shut, and my eyes widened. Shadow Pack? The room seemed to spin around me. The stories I'd heard as a child, the legends, they were real?

"Is this what Rowan has been keeping from us? What you

—and you—?" I pointed at Lana and Callista. They both nodded. "So there's another realm. An entire mystical pack. And you're using that power to try and find the relics—"

"And the Northern Alphas who are using them against the wolves in our territory," Lana clarified. "They are calling to us. The prophecy says that they will be reunited, but we can't allow them to be used again as they were anciently. It would lead to the destruction of us all, not only Shadow Pack."

Like it did the first time. I'd heard the stories of Thorne Moreau, but I thought it was a value tale. Something to keep us from being power hungry and selfish. All of it actually happened?

"Holy shit." I ran my fingers through my hair.

"My thoughts exactly," Liam muttered.

A call. Erin. The fire. The relics. My brain worked to connect all the dots, and it started giving me a headache.

After a few deep breaths, I looked up. "If you can't find them with Shadow Pack magic, what the hell are we supposed to do?"

Lana glanced up at Destin. "I still think they must be there. In the center."

"*Of the fire?*" I blurted.

The corner of Destin's mouth curled. "Get comfy. This is going to be hot as hell."

CHAPTER

TWELVE

CONNOR

So. They were hiding shit.

I ducked behind the corner of the house as soon as I saw them moving toward the door. The whole group of them had been in the bedroom I used last night. Plain as day through the slight gap in the curtains. Which made me instantly think of Mia on the porch last night. She'd been sitting there while I was changing.

What was it about her? She seemed to take up more residence in my head with every passing hour, which wasn't like me. I hadn't dated since Lydia and I split. Not seriously anyway. I was focused solely on Elle, on trying to be as much a part of her life as Lydia would let me be.

But now I didn't have that excuse. My body certainly knew it. And my mind. Considering how often that image of Mia in my bed flashed through my thoughts.

I started walking to keep my blood flowing in more than one direction and forced myself to focus. What were they meeting about? Why all the secrecy? Mia said they didn't have any information on the fire, and while it was possible that they were problem solving the situation with Mia's sister, it seemed like more than that.

I stalked toward the command tent. Voices sounded from the cabin, and I quickened my pace, the flap of the tent brushing against my arm as I stepped inside.

"Connor!" a voice called out, followed by the sound of chairs scraping against the floor. I turned to see my team. Damn, we were a rough and tumble bunch.

"If you're taking a break, you may as well shower," I grumbled. "I didn't realize we were running a resort here."

Marco looked up from the bag of chips in his hand. "Hey, Chief. We were waiting for you. Line's about to swap out."

My heart swelled a little. The guys respected me just as I respected them. But I loved that they also saw me as a father figure, and not because I was old and crotchety. Well, maybe a little crotchety. Definitely not old.

Tiff walked in, and when she looked up, a hint of a smirk played on her lips. "Well, well, well," she said, her voice sharp and teasing. "Look what we've got here. The great Connor Bastien, slumming it with the common folk."

I grinned. "Good morning to you."

She walked over, her eyes narrowing as she looked at me. "Morning started three hours ago. You look like hell."

I shrugged. "Tired, that's all."

Tiff raised an eyebrow. "Huh. That's all, eh?"

"What else could it be? Life here is peachy keen."

Tiff's mouth twitched. "Okay, then." She turned to the team. "Let's get out there."

We geared up and relieved blue team who'd been working

since four in the morning. They were exhausted. I may have shamelessly sent a few of them looking for Sue's shower.

We got to work. Pushing my body until my muscles screamed was the best thing I could've done. It took my head out of the equation, and for seven hours plus a lunch break, I was exactly who I'd been up until I'd found Mia trespassing in the data trailer.

I didn't like that I felt different. Didn't like that I was thinking about her or feeling off-kilter. Something was wrong. But at least while I was swinging a chain saw, I didn't have to think about it.

After grunting our goodnights, I returned to my trailer exhausted. I couldn't think in full sentences, and I was salivating at the idea of a microwavable freezer meal.

Just as it should be.

Back to ground zero.

But as my fingers hit the handle to my trailer, I froze. Movement. Just past the edge of the trees. I squinted, trying to get a better look. It was too high off the ground to be an animal. Most of them had fled from the smoke.

I should've turned around. I should've pulled the door open and walked inside. Microwaved my meal, taken a piddly shower in the trailer and crashed.

But I'd been doing "should've" for seven years, and I couldn't stand the idea of towing the line for one second longer.

CHAPTER

THIRTEEN

MIA

Liam walked next to me through the trees, his arms crossed over his chest. "I don't like this. The Shadow Realm? What was it they said existed there? Bone Watchers?"

"Stalkers. And they can appear in our world, too, so it's not like I'm taking any additional risk." I stepped over a branch, nearly tripping when I misjudged the height. Wolf eyes were good at night, but I hadn't let mine run for weeks. She was annoyed, which meant she was holding back. I couldn't blame her.

Soon. I promise. I couldn't risk shifting yet. Not until I was far from Connor Bastien.

Liam laughed. "Right. Definitely no risk."

We stopped when we reached the stream. That's where Lana and Destin had asked us to meet them. "I don't know,

77

Liam. What Lana said . . . I think she's right. Maybe there's a reason I was called here. Maybe Erin's not stuck with the fire, maybe she's in trouble."

The thought sent a swoop through my belly. I always used to know when Erin was in trouble.

I was instantly back in our childhood bedroom, waking to the sound of Erin whimpering in her sleep. The room was dark, save for the dim glow of the moon pushing weakly through the thin curtains. Erin let out a soft, broken noise, her body curled into a tight ball beneath the blankets.

I pushed back my own covers, the old wooden floor creaking beneath my weight as I slid from my bed to hers. She was trembling, her breath uneven, and when I reached out to touch her arm, I felt it.

Her nightmare crashed into me like a wave—thick shadows curling from the walls, skeletal hands reaching, gnarled fingers dragging against the floor. A figure with a face I couldn't see, its mouth stretched too wide, whispering something I couldn't understand.

Erin's fear hit me like a sharp sting to my chest, an electric pulse of panic that tried to dig into my bones. I inhaled. Pulling the darkness into me.

It wasn't real.

I pressed my forehead to hers, my fingers curling against her wrist.

"Erin," I whispered, my voice steady. *"It's not real."*

Her breath hitched. The nightmare curled tighter, refusing to release its hold.

So I showed her. I let her feel what I felt.

Calm. Steady. Control.

Erin let out a shaky breath, her body relaxing beneath my touch. The room shifted—the shadows flickered and retreated, pulling away from the corners, dissolving into nothing.

Her fear bled into me, filling the spaces between my ribs, but I held it. I always did. Just as she did for me.

Erin's fingers curled into my sleeve, her voice a whisper. *"You saw it?"*

I nodded, shifting under the blanket with her, keeping my hand wrapped around her wrist. We never questioned it. I saw her nightmares. She saw mine. We'd always shared them, always pulled each other out.

I stared at the ceiling, my heart still hammering.

"Go back to sleep," I murmured. She was my older sister. But in moments like that, we were equals.

"Why would Erin be connected to any of it? With the alpha's? A relic?" Liam shook his head. "I don't see how that's possible."

"Yeah, well, we're not really ones to talk to about impossible things." I pressed my palm against the rough bark of the tree next to me, my fingers tracing the grooves. "Like Lana said. We go in. If we don't find anything, then—"

"She's already been in there. She couldn't find them. Why would you think you could?"

I swallowed hard. I'd been asking myself the same question all afternoon. Lana wanted me to come. She knew about my connection with Erin. She thought it might be a lead we could follow. "I probably can't. So I'll see you for a late dinner."

Liam exhaled, his shoulders slumping. "I didn't mean it like that." He shoved his hands in his pockets. "I don't want anything to happen to you."

I nodded, my throat tight. Liam had accompanied me on a wild goose chase without hesitation. He'd slept on the fire chief's table bed. Now he was helping the crews with wildfire containment. He was my friend, and he had a heart of gold. "Liam, I promise I'll be careful. But know that I'm just as worried about you every time you walk out in that fire gear."

He glanced up. "Who would've thought. Me. Using power tools."

I laughed out loud. "Speaking of which, isn't your shift starting?"

"Yeah." He nodded, scuffing his boots over the forest mulch. "See you for dinner then."

I grinned. "I'll fail as fast as possible."

As if on cue, Lana and Destin appeared from the trees. Kael and Callista followed close after. Liam gave a small wave, then ducked back into the shadow of the woods.

Lana motioned for us all to move closer together. "I'm not going to waste time with small talk. Since none of you are Shadow Pack, I have to pull you through. You all have to stay connected. Once we're there, stay close. We move together, we watch each other's backs."

I nodded along with the others.

We clasped hands, Lana gripping Kael's shoulder, and the world around us seemed to hold its breath. She led us forward, the darkness swallowing us whole.

And it was in that moment that my arm yanked backward, my body flying off-balance. I cried out as my skin went cold and the woods swirled in my vision. Then I was flat on my back with my ribs crushed against my spine.

Because Connor Bastien lay on top of me.

CHAPTER

FOURTEEN

CONNOR

I didn't think. I just moved.

I lunged forward and reached for Mia as soon as her form began to fade. Alarm bells clanged in my head. This didn't make any sense—what I'd just witnessed didn't make any sense.

And then I was lying flat. Pressed against—

"Connor?" Mia shoved against my shoulders, pushing me off of her with enough force, I landed on my ass.

I scanned the area around us. *What the hell happened?* One second, I was standing in the clearing, the next, I was . . . somewhere else. The air felt heavier here, like I was breathing through a wet blanket. The trees were still there, but they looked different—twisted, ghostly.

I scrambled up from the spongy ground to find the others staring at me, their faces a mix of shock and horror. Lana's

81

mouth was hanging open, and Destin's face darkened like a thundercloud.

"Shit," Lana muttered, turning away from me.

Mia stood next to me, brushing off her jeans. "Send him back. There has to be some way—"

Kael moved without warning, his massive frame lunging toward me with a speed that belied his size. His gray eyes were hard, his jaw set in a grim line. His intent was clear. Of course he wasn't thrilled that I'd tagged along to their occult party.

But I wasn't going down without a fight.

My body reacted before my mind could catch up, my instincts kicking in with a raw, primal intensity. I twisted to the side, avoiding his initial blow by mere inches. His fist grazed my shoulder, the force of it sending a sharp sting through my arm. But I didn't have time to register the pain. I was already moving, my hands curling into fists as I spun back around to face him.

He came at me again, but I was ready. I'd taken martial arts through high school and college. I was a little rusty, but with my size advantage, I ducked under his next punch, my heart sounding off in my chest, and countered with a sharp jab to his ribs. The impact was solid. He grunted, his breath hitching, but he didn't stop. How the hell did he keep coming back for more?

"Enough," Destin growled. Kael froze.

I stood in front of him, panting with my fists raised. "What is this place?"

Lana took a step forward, her eyes flashing. "You shouldn't be here."

Before I could process the surreal horror around me, a figure emerged from the shadows. He was tall, with black hair that fell to his shoulders and luminous eyes that seemed to bore into my soul.

The group around me stiffened, holding their collective breath.

Lana stepped forward, her dark hair swinging with the motion. Her eyes were sharp, her jaw set in a determined line. "Gabriel, we did not bring him here on purpose."

Gabriel? Every Christmas mass I'd attended as a kid came flooding back into my memory. Was I dead? Had I only been dreaming about the clearing, and somehow the Gabriel spoken of in the bible was darker than I'd imagined?

I was losing my grip on reality. The world around me was a twisted parody of the one I knew, and the longer I stood there, the more my mind struggled to make sense of it.

Lana's jaw tightened, and her arm snapped out, grabbing onto me and dragging me forward. My first instinct was to fight like I had with Kael, but unless she hit me first, I wasn't going to lash out. It went against everything in me to hit a woman.

There was a jolt of something—electric, sharp—and then she gasped, pulling back as if burned. Lana looked up at Destin, then back at me, her eyes wide. "I can't take him back."

"What?" Mia looked as if someone had just run over her cat.

I motioned around us at the lazy fog curling in the other-worldly light. "I'm waiting for an explanation."

Lana swallowed hard, and for a moment, I thought she might lunge at me. But then she deflated, her shoulders sagging as she let out a sharp breath. "Fine. You want answers? You're in the Shadow Realm. It's a place between worlds. A thin veil. Happy?"

I clenched my jaw. No. I sure as hell wasn't happy. None of what she'd just said made sense to me. "Am I dead?"

Kael snorted. "I wish."

"Hey." Mia stepped forward, and I took a step back. Rage radiated from her in waves. "Why were you watching us?"

"You were meeting secretly. Not too hard to figure—"

"Secretly? We're allowed to speak with our friends privately without worrying that community leaders lead double lives as Peeping Tom's."

"That's not—"

"Isn't it?" She raised an eyebrow, planting her hands on her hips. She let out a growl that somehow seemed frustrated and apologetic. Not to me. She was pissed at me. Clearly. "We're here because—" She hesitated, her gaze flicking to the others before settling back on me. "Because we have to be."

I crossed my arms over my chest, doing what I did with my team every time we had to suit up and go into a blaze. Putting on my armor. Because I sure as hell wasn't going to let her skate around my question with a piss-poor answer like that.

"I'm looking at a pale-ass version of the woods and just got chastised by a frigging arch angel. Answer the damn question, Mia."

Lana had spoken gibberish, but I still had no idea what this place was. Mia didn't cower. Instead she stalked forward, her eyes flashing. All five-foot-six of her looking ready to explode. "I don't owe you anything."

Her eyes shone golden, something flickering there that I'd never seen before. My breath left my lungs in a whoosh. "You're not human." The realization hit me like a punch to the gut. Everything in me wanted to deny it. Wanted to tell myself I was imagining things, that I was sleep-deprived, exhausted, that the wildfire smoke was messing with my head.

But it wasn't.

Smoke filled my vision. Flashing lights.

I wasn't there for her. Elle. Members of my team had seen her burns, and by the time I got to her, sick with worry, I'd held her in my arms. Cried like a baby. And when they lifted her bandages . . . Nothing could've prepared me or the doctors for that moment.

They couldn't explain it. Her skin was perfect. Unmarred. We'd walked home like nothing had happened, but I couldn't let it go. I'd put my team through the third degree and only pulled one piece of helpful information. A woman. At the ambulance.

I tried to rationalize it. Tried to tell myself it had been luck, a miracle, excellent medical responders. But then I found out it was Mia's mother at the ambulance. Why the hell would she have been there? Her own home was burning. It made no sense.

I had gone to their house, knocked on the door. No answer. Went again, a few days later. Still nothing.

When I finally caught Mia's father outside, I tried to explain—tried to tell him I needed to know what happened that night. He tried to tell me my team was mistaken.

Now, I don't believe fire fighters are perfect. But when it comes to remembering details, they're pretty damn close.

Now, staring at Mia's golden eyes, it all slammed together like a puzzle I'd spent too long ignoring. There was something else at play. Something I didn't understand.

I dragged a hand down my face. I'd spent years trying to tell myself there had to be a logical explanation. But believing in magic made a hell of a lot more sense than whatever else I'd spent the last decade trying to convince myself of.

Lana's jaw tightened, but she didn't deny it. "We're not entirely human, no. We're shifters."

I stared at her, my mind racing. Shifters. "You change shape?"

"Wolf shifters," Kael grunted.

Right. Wolves. So much easier to understand. I almost laughed. It sounded like something out of a bad horror movie,

My eyes locked onto Mia's. She stood there, still jutting out her chin. I took a step closer. "Is that what you are?"

"She's—" Lana started, but I cut her off.

"No. I want to hear it from her." She'd been in my house—she'd stayed with Elle alone. Anger flared in me like a lit pilot light, and I couldn't seem to tamp it down.

"I'm a shifter. Yes."

I ground my teeth. "Let me see it."

Mia scoffed. "Hell, no."

"Mia—"

"Okay, show and tell is over." Lana stormed forward, pulling Mia back next to her. "Apparently, you can't leave this realm, but do not think for one second I won't tie your ass to a chair."

"That's probably one of his fantasies," Kael quipped, and Callista rolled her eyes.

Destin cleared his throat. "He should come with us."

Lana whirled on him like he'd just stepped on her tail. "What?"

"He knows fire."

"We're in the Shadow Realm."

Destin walked forward and cupped her face in his hands, breathing until her shoulders dropped an inch. "And we may have to leave it." He leaned in and murmured something in her ear.

I dropped my eyes. The whole thing seemed strangely intimate, and despite being accused of it, I wasn't a Peeping Tom.

Lana nodded, then turned to face me. "You will stay close. Or I'll put you in that chair. And not in a hot way."

CHAPTER

FIFTEEN

Mɪᴀ

Lana disappeared momentarily, and when she returned, she was no longer holding the book. Made sense. If it was as precious as she said, there was no way I'd want to take it any closer to one of the alphas. *If we found them.*

We linked together and moved through the Shadow Realm with cautious steps. Gabriel, Lana, and Destin stood on the other end of the line, and Connor pulled up the rear after me. The ground beneath our feet was spongy when we touched it, but it almost felt like we glided above it. The sky overhead was a swirling vortex of grays and blacks, the ghosts of trees, hills and rocks buzzing by like we had the pedal to the floor on a backroad highway.

Connor's hand wrapped around mine, and it wasn't until we stopped the third time that I noticed his palm felt cold. I

87

glanced over, not wanting him to notice I was looking. I shouldn't have worried. His eyes were focused straight ahead, his jaw clenched.

His shoulders were hunched, and his hair was damp, clinging to his forehead.

"Are you okay?" I asked.

He shot me a look. "Fine."

But a moment later, he stumbled, and I held him upright. "You're not fine," I hissed, then called out for Lana.

She and Gabriel left our formation and walked over, their eyes sweeping over him.

"Humans are not made for this realm," Gabriel murmured.

Lana nodded. "You think it's affecting him."

"I know it is."

My brow furrowed. "But he can't leave? That makes no sense."

Gabriel's expression was grim. "It will only get worse." He turned and walked away as if he hadn't just pronounced a death sentence.

There was nothing else to do but keep moving. Darkness swirled in the center of the strange images around us. Fire. We were engulfed in it and couldn't feel a thing.

Connor coughed, and I turned to him. "What were you thinking?"

He shrugged, his expression brooding. "I had to know what was going on. I couldn't just sit back and do nothing."

"You could've asked."

He blew out a breath that sounded like it was supposed to be a laugh. "And you would've answered?"

No. I wouldn't have, and he knew it. But now he was standing here deteriorating next to me. My ribs felt like they'd shrunk two sizes in the wash. Why did I care? It was his stupid decision, and now I was worrying about him?

Connor grunted. "I can handle it."

"You're not handling it very well," I snapped. I thought my commentary was going to end there, but it didn't. "You always try to tell people what to do, and you don't give explanations, yet you're not willing to listen unless you get all the details."

"I need all the details. It's how I keep people safe."

I scoffed. "Right. And somehow you have more right to keep people safe than anyone else? If you wouldn't have forced us to stay in your trailer—"

"If you would've told me you were a wolf shifter, I wouldn't have."

My jaw dropped. "Mm. Nice. I'm sure that would've gone over well. Slip it in there between the trespassing accusations and microwave meals."

Connor yanked me closer to him. "If you want to be pissed at me, be pissed at me. But you have information that could've helped with this fire, and you withheld it."

"I had nothing! I came to find my sister. You know as much as I do at this point." Not exactly true, but close enough.

Connor didn't argue back. Probably because he was coughing so hard he could barely breathe.

As we continued through the realm, the atmosphere grew heavier. Connor's struggles became more pronounced, his steps faltering, his body shivering.

I hated it. Every second.

When we finally made it into the eye of the storm and stopped, I exhaled in relief. Which made no sense because we still didn't have a way to get him the hell out of there.

I dropped Connor's hand and scanned the area. "This is it?"

Lana nodded and stepped out with Gabriel. The walked the perimeter, murmuring to each other and looking for something. I searched for any sign of life, any indication that there was an alpha or a relic on the other side of this strange realm. And, if I was being honest, any sign of my sister.

"We rest here. Not long, but we'll need our strength when we figure out where they're hiding." Lana strode back to us. She didn't raise her hand or make any outward motion, but suddenly the air filled with the aroma of food, rich and inviting. Beds with fresh, clean linens sprung out of the ground, their posts woven with ivy and flowers.

I stared, mesmerized by the beauty of it. When I reached out a hand for a piece of fruit, Destin stopped me. "Be careful with that."

I frowned. "What do you mean?"

Lana nudged him. "This is different. I asked for it."

He looked at the table, then at Lana. Her cheeks flamed red. What the hell was that all about?

I looked back and found Connor already collapsed on one of the beds. I traipsed over and stood next to him. "You should eat something."

He rolled to his side but didn't open his eyes. "I'm not hungry."

He was pale. Curling his knees into his chest, his whole body shivering. And for a moment, I no longer saw him as Connor the fire chief. He was just a man. A human. Suffering.

Liam would never have let this stand.

I walked back to the table and made a plate with rolls, cheeses, fruit, and smoked meats, then strode back to the bed. I sat on the mattress next to him.

"Don't make me spill this on your shirt." When he didn't answer, I nudged his shoulder. His eyes flickered, and my stomach dropped out from under me. "Connor, seriously. You should eat something."

He shook his head, and I set down the plate, moving further onto the bed. I put a hand on his cheek, patting lightly. "Connor, if you have a fantasy of me feeding you by hand—"

"Stop it, Mia."

I pressed my palm to his face. Holy shit, he was cold. "No. I'm not going to stop. You need to eat something." I picked up a piece of what looked like chicken and held it to his lips. Reluctantly, he opened his mouth and let me put it on his tongue. He chewed, weakly, but after a moment, it looked like he swallowed.

His eyelids lifted. "That was good."

The corner of my mouth curled. "I slaved over a hot stove—"

"Just give me another bite."

I fed him as much as I could before exhaustion overtook him again, at least managing to get some water in him, too. I finished the rest of the plate and stood only to find the others gone. The table, the other beds—all except for one that must've been meant for me—disappeared. I couldn't find any of it in the thick mist that had gathered while we'd been eating.

"Fantastic," I muttered, then turned back to find our plate was nonexistent. Well. It seemed my work here was done. I turned and started toward my bed, then paused. He was still shivering.

Damn it. I was going to kill Liam for planting his voice in my head.

I climbed back onto the bed and worked at Connor's shirt. My babysitter training of all things popped into my head. If someone is hypothermic, you strip them down and use body heat to warm them up. I doubted that was in anyone's curriculum south of the border, but up here, it was drilled into our heads a thousand times. That and "always have a quilt and two meals in the trunk of your car."

Severe cases needed direct skin contact. Clothes held moisture, and moisture leached heat away from the body. It was basic survival. I knew this.

Didn't make it less awkward.

Connor wasn't conscious enough to help or argue, which made this ten times harder. His frame was massive, his shoulders broad enough that rolling him took half my strength, especially since my wolf was on hiatus. "Come on, big guy," I gritted out, wrestling his shirt up over his chest. The fabric clung, damp with sweat and lingering cold.

His body radiated tension, even in sleep. Like his muscles were braced for something, even as he shivered uncontrollably. I managed to peel his shirt off, hanging it on one of the posts. His skin was warm in places, clammy in others—inconsistent heat, a bad sign.

I hesitated.

I wasn't exactly thrilled about what I had to do next.

But it wasn't like I had a choice.

Gritting my teeth, I pulled my own shirt over my head, stripping down to bare skin and my bra. The air felt cooler against my back, making the contrast sharper as I slid beneath the quilt.

Connor was huge, which meant getting him under the blankets with me was a battle. I braced one knee against the mattress, grabbed his deadweight-heavy arm, and hauled. He barely budged.

"Oh, for—" I exhaled sharply, maneuvering onto my side and pressing my chest against his. Finally, I was able to yank the sheets and quilt out from under him. I flopped down to the mattress, then reached back and dragged the quilt over us, shifting until I was flush against him.

My heart pounded against my ribs.

From the effort.

At least, that's what I told myself.

Connor let out a low sigh, then reached over his side and grabbed my wrist, pulling it over him and wrapping his hand over mine.

Not sure if that was a subconscious reaction or not, but my heart rate kicking up a notch definitely wasn't. His back pressed against my chest, my stomach, with every inhale, and he somehow pulled me closer with every exhale.

I had nowhere to put my head. If I lay it on my pillow, I had to crane my neck. Finally, I gave up and nestled my cheek against his shoulder. Somehow, despite the stress he was under, he still smelled good. Like sun kissed skin and warm spice.

I swallowed hard and tried to focus on mechanics, on the logic of the situation. This was textbook first aid. It didn't matter that his body was solid, all muscle and broad warmth beneath my palms. Didn't matter that I was keenly aware of every inch of skin pressed against mine.

What mattered was keeping him alive and getting his body temperature back up. I exhaled slowly, trying to ignore the way my pulse tripped in my throat.

Ugh. I hated myself a little for being such a good person.

CHAPTER
SIXTEEN

CONNOR

The second her skin hit mine, I was wide awake. I wouldn't admit it, but the food helped. The shivering felt more like an after-effect than my body's desperate attempt to warm me.

Guilt niggled at me. Mia was only lying next to me because she thought I was in danger, and here I was, taking advantage of it. I couldn't stop myself from reaching out and pulling her arm around me.

I may not have been desperate for heat, but I was desperate for this. I didn't even know it until she was there, her skin pressed against mine. I hated feeling weak, but if this was the reward, I might consider looking at it more often.

In that moment, the looks we shared and the strange pull I felt toward her solidified into something more than passing thoughts I'd been trying to bury for the past forty-eight hours. As wrong as it looked on paper, I was attracted to her. More than I had been to any woman in the past ten years. I loved how she fit against me, the way her curves molded to my frame, but it was a comfort I was ashamed to enjoy.

I hadn't earned her compassion, and she hadn't earned my trust. She'd hidden this from me—from everyone in Kitimat and Black Lake. Those old wounds of betrayal broke open even though Mia hadn't made me any promises.

"You're a stubborn ass," Mia whispered, her cheek nestled against my bare shoulder, her breath whispering over my neck.

"Did I pretend to be otherwise?" I whispered back. Her body tensed in surprise, and I grinned. She thought I was asleep.

My shivering slowed again, but I purposefully kept it up. Just so she wouldn't pull away too quickly.

"You were different. Back then."

I drew a breath and slowly exhaled. "I didn't know who I was. Maybe I still don't." Where had that come from? I hadn't admitted that to myself, let alone to someone else. It was something about this place. It had knocked me down. Cracked me open. With every soft shift of her body, my insides seemed to ooze out.

"What will you do? Now that you know?" Mia's voice was soft.

I considered the question, but it didn't take long for me to reply, "Know what?" I wasn't being facetious. Yes, I was in a strange realm. Yes, I'd heard from their own mouths that they had magical abilities. But what did that mean? I couldn't even begin to think through the ramifications.

"You know about us." Mia's fingers twitched under mine.

Us. *Them.* My brain went into problem-solving mode. As

much as it could with my head still foggy and slow. I started with step one. Power that I couldn't explain existed. *Magic.* I sat with that momentarily, then tore up everything I knew about the world and rewrote it.

"How does it work?" I asked.

Mia swallowed, her cheek moving against my skin. "Which part?"

"All of it. Does everyone in your family have this ability?"

"Yes. And everyone in our pack."

Pack. That word sounded feral. I thought back to my interactions with Mia's family, with their friends or people I saw them with in the community. "Rowan. He's your . . . leader. Or something like that."

Mia nodded against my shoulder. "Alpha. It used to be Nathan Black."

I frowned. "I haven't seen him in a while. Did he—"

"He's dead."

My mouth opened and closed. Dead? "How?"

"It doesn't matter. I don't miss him. I don't think any of us do."

Her tone was bitter. I didn't view Nathan as a crowd-pleaser, but it sounded like there was more to the story than I'd casually observed.

Mia pulled her arm back, but I held on, keeping her there. Just a moment longer. I knew the second she left, this spell between us would break. She'd go back to keeping her secrets, and I'd go back to . . . what? To fighting fires? To texting Elle and eating microwave dinners? Mia's life hadn't changed, but mine? It was altered forever.

"You can't talk about this with anyone," she murmured. "Promise me you won't—"

"I can't promise you that."

Mia yanked her hand back and rolled away from me. Even

though I'd stopped shivering, my body shuddered at the loss of her. "You don't understand," she muttered, her voice barely audible. "We've been hunted for centuries. If humans find out about us, they'll come with torches and pitchforks. They always do."

I rolled to my back and turned my head, forcing her to meet my gaze. "Not all humans. Some of us aren't afraid. But how would you figure that out when you're too busy hiding."

Mia ran her hands through her hair, frustration curling her fingers tight. "There's a reason we keep our secrets."

I rolled to my side, watching her in the dim light, the golden glow in her eyes still simmering beneath the surface. My body had finally warmed, but a different heat settled in now.

She didn't get it.

She thought she had humans all figured out. Thought she could lump me in with the rest of them—people who feared what they didn't understand. But I'd been trained with fear as a constant companion. And fire was magic to me.

I exhaled sharply. "So what? I'm supposed to pretend I never saw any of this?"

"That would be ideal."

"Too late."

She glared at me. Damn, she was furious. It did something to me, that sharp intensity, the way her anger burned hot and fast.

"You've known about this for all of ten minutes," she snapped. "And you think you're somehow an ally?"

"Why wouldn't I be?" I shot back.

She let out a bitter laugh, sharp as a blade. "That's not how this works. You don't know what it's like to live with a target on your back."

I pushed myself up onto my elbow, leaning in. "You don't

know what it's like to watch a fire consume everything you love and realize there's nothing you can do to stop it."

Her jaw tightened, but she didn't look away.

"People like me—we run toward the danger," I said. "Not away from it."

Mia scoffed. "Oh, so now you think you're some kind of noble hero?"

"Not a hero," I said. "Just not a coward."

That did it.

Her eyes flashed molten gold, and before I could react, she shoved me. I wasn't expecting it. I grabbed onto the sheets, yanking them toward me as I righted myself.

And then my mouth went dry. She was right there in front of me, breathing hard, her chest rising and falling, the straps of her bra stark against her bare skin.

Oh, hell.

I tried not to be too obvious, tried to keep my gaze some-where neutral, but there was no neutral here. Just Mia, all soft curves and sharp edges, glowing like something untouchable and wild.

I swallowed hard. Didn't help.

Her brows lifted, amusement flickering through the anger. "See something you like, Chief?"

Damn her. I tore my gaze away, clenching my jaw, forcing my body to behave. Not easy when every single nerve was suddenly screaming at me to close the space between us. I cleared my throat and threw the blankets back to her side. "That was your fault."

Her smirk deepened. She knew exactly what I'd been think-ing. And I hated how much I liked her knowing.

"Your arrogance isn't my fault." Instead of pulling the quilt back over her, she sat up, daring me to look.

My eyes had barely trailed over her collarbone when I

heard it. A low, rumbling growl. The sound rippled through the dark, raising the hairs on my arms.

Mia went rigid. My instincts kicked in immediately—my body moving before my brain caught up. I reached for her, flipping her to her side and curling her against my chest, shielding her beneath me as I turned toward the sound.

CHAPTER

SEVENTEEN

MIA

The moment Connor moved over me, sheltering me with his body, pressing his heat against me, I forgot how to breathe.

I should have shoved him away, should have reminded him that I was the one who should be protecting him in this scenario, but I didn't move. I let him cover me. And that was a mistake. Because now? Now, I couldn't think of anything but him.

His weight pinned me down, not crushing, but in a way that made me feel small—protected. His body was too warm, too solid, and I could feel every inch of him, from the tense muscles in his arms to the steady press of his chest against my back.

I swallowed, my pulse thundering in my ears. I shouldn't be reacting like this. But I was. And the worst part? I knew he felt it, too. I could still see how his gaze had caught on me before, how he had tried to look away when the blanket had fallen, and how his breath had hitched just a second too long.

He wanted me.

I was still pissed that he'd followed us here and terrified that he didn't seem to understand how much power he held over me and the rest of my pack. But that tiny bit of knowledge sent a dark thrill racing through me, something hot and dangerous curling in my stomach.

Because I shouldn't want him back. I was an adult, but he. Was. An. Adult. Ten years older than me? And human?

But my body? My body had other ideas. I bit the inside of my cheek, forcing myself to stay still.

We weren't alone. There was something out there, watching us. My mind flew back to Liam in the trees, talking about Bone Stalkers. Did they growl? I instantly regretted not asking Lana more questions.

Connor stayed perfectly still above me, his muscles locked. He was waiting. Listening. I should have been doing the same. But my mind wouldn't stop racing.

We were in danger, and Connor shouldn't be here. Not in the Shadow Realm. Not with me. What if he returned to his life and realized he couldn't let it go? Or worse—what if he never made it out at all?

I clenched my jaw. I didn't want to think about that or the possibility of Connor being trapped here forever, hunted by things he didn't understand.

I tensed at the sound of a low, sharp voice. "Are you insane?" Destin. Even though I couldn't see him through the mist, I knew it was him.

"I saw it, and I have to do something about it," Lana snapped.

"He'll feel you instantly."

I relaxed, blood rushing in my ears. We weren't in danger,

but now I didn't dare move. How close were they? *Would they see us like this?*

"Lana," Destin's voice was pleading.

"I don't have a choice. I'm . . . receiving more."

Destin paused. "What?"

I closed my eyes, Connor's heartbeat drowning out any comprehension of their words.

"They're coming faster," Lana said. "Not just through the relics anymore, and you heard what Gabriel said. The Shadow Pack is coming alive. If there are more out there, maybe they're sharing."

Destin exhaled. They had to be close if I could hear that. I turned my head, my pulse thrumming so loud, I could barely hear what Lana said next. " . . . it can only be broken by blood, and you know who . . . "

I waited, still pinned beneath Connor, until their voices faded completely, then sank into the mattress with a sigh. We weren't in danger, but the second we'd gone into high alert, Connor—human and vulnerable and weak—had immediately put himself between me and the threat.

My chest squeezed. Who does that? Who protects a predator?

The moment that thought crossed my mind, my wolf surged forward violently and without warning. I gasped, my body tensing as heat rushed through me, a sharp, over-whelming pulse of desire and something deeper—something primal.

I'd barely felt her all week. She'd been quiet, distant. But now she was wide awake and alive. And she was focused on him.

My breath hitched as my back arched involuntarily, pressing me tighter against Connor. Every nerve in my body became a live wire as she pushed toward him, scenting him, inspecting him. The sensation was overwhelming, like drowning in warm, liquid fire. I felt his heartbeat, the heat of his skin, and his breath against my cheek.

Connor let out a sharp, unsteady breath, his fingers tightening slightly against my waist. My body moved on its own, my hips shifting just enough to brush against him, my mouth parting as a shudder rippled through me.

What the hell was happening? I tried to drag myself out of the tide, but the pull was too strong. And then I was moving. I barely even realized it, the way my lips found the inside of his arm, the way my mouth brushed over the skin there, warm and soft and searching.

A low, rumbling sound left Connor's throat, something halfway between a sigh and a groan. His breath was uneven, his body tense.

"Mia." He dropped his head, and I finally surfaced.

Oh. Oh gods.

I froze, then jerked back, my heart slamming against my ribs as I scrambled out from under him. Connor was panting, his face tight, his pupils blown wide.

"I—" His voice was hoarse, raw, like he hadn't spoken in hours. "I think whatever that was is gone."

I nodded once, then launched away from him, horrified.

No, no, no. This was not happening. This wasn't how things worked. I was a shifter. He was human.

What the hell was that? I demanded mentally.

My wolf stretched lazily, unconcerned. *Instinct.*

INSTINCT?! I practically screamed inside my head. *You just—*

We like him, she purred.

I nearly choked on air. *We do NOT like him.*

She flicked her tail. *You're lying to yourself. He is strong. He protects. He desires us. You felt it. He would be—*

You missed one crucial detail. I cut her off, staggering away from the bed, my pulse still a mess. *He's human!*

She was silent for a moment. Then she murmured, *He's different.*

I didn't want to hear it.

I frantically searched the ground for my shirt, my hands shaking as I yanked it over my head. Connor's gaze was still on me, burning into my skin, but I couldn't look at him.

Not after that. Not after I had lost all semblance of control and started *kissing him.* I barely mumbled an excuse before darting back to my bed.

A flash of color cut through the endless gray of the Shadow Realm, jarring in its vibrancy.

I froze. My embarrassment from a few moments before evaporated as my wolf snapped to attention, letting out a low growl. I crept closer, then dropped to my knees with a gasp.

A small, jewel-toned clutch rested in the murky land-scape like an impossible beacon. My stomach twisted violently. I knew that purse. Erin's favorite. The one she'd saved up for months to buy, the one she had babied like a cherished pet. The inside joke we had about it—her "adult lady purse."

What the hell was it doing here?

Erin couldn't be in the Shadow Realm. She couldn't be. But if she was with the alphas . . . Ice crawled through my veins. I tried to snatch it up, but my trembling fingers passed through it like a mirage.

I whirled around, voice cracking. "Lana! Lana, I found something!"

Within seconds, the mist began to clear, and Lana appeared across the clearing, lying next to Destin. She shot upright, hand already on the dagger, her sharp eyes scanning the darkness. "What is it? What's wrong?"

I pointed at the purse, my hand still shaking. "It's Erin's. She's here. Somehow."

Lana's expression went stone cold. She gave Destin a look as he rubbed the sleep from his eyes. "I saw nothing."

He nodded once, then threw his legs off the side of the bed. Gabriel appeared between them. "What is it?" He directed the question to Lana, but I turned to him, forcing the words out past the dread coiling in my gut.

"I found this." I pointed at the purse.

Lana strode toward it, crouching down. "It doesn't make sense. There aren't any signs of habitation here. I haven't seen one person—"

"You can see them?" Connor stepped up beside me. Good. He was wearing a shirt.

Lana nodded. "They can't see us, but yes. We can typically hear them, too."

I worried my lower lip. Was it possible she'd dropped this here? The idea made no sense. That it would be sitting in the middle of the woods—in the middle of a wildfire—unscathed?

Gabriel gave Lana a look. "You believe they're using the amulet."

Lana blew out a breath and stood from her crouch. "You think it's capable of this?"

Gabriel frowned. "I do not know everything about the relics after the breaking. Their power is twisted. But you've read The Book of Shadows—"

"It may allow them to mask more than just their scent," Kael mused, appearing next to Destin with Callista.

Lana nodded. "We can't trust what we see here." She planted her hands on her hips and turned in a circle.

"If they've bonded with the relic, other powers may be at play. We can't move out of this realm without knowing what they are," Kael continued.

Lana tapped the dagger resting at her hip. "Maybe it's the same," she mused.

Mia frowned. "The same as what?"

Callista's eyes narrowed. "You think the amulet may be stopped?"

Lana gave a half-hearted shrug. "I don't know."

Connor exhaled. "Explanation, please."

Lana looked mildly apologetic. "A dear friend gave his blood to the dagger. A willing sacrifice. It removed the curse from Callista. And the book . . . " She met Destin's eye.

"That required sacrifice," he murmured.

She nodded. "Not the same, though. The amulet may ask for something else entirely."

Kael ran his hand through his hair. "And you think it will put a stop to this?"

Callista frowned. "If there's a way to stop it, we can't stay here. Not if we want to learn anything."

"They know our wolves," Kael argued. "If they can shield their presence here, they may already have sensed our approach."

Lana shook her head. "No, that's not how the Shadow Realm works. They may be able to shield themselves from us, but they can't access this realm alone. Not without Shadow Pack."

My stomach twisted. "What if they have one?"

Lana's brow furrowed. "Shadow Pack?"

I nodded. "They've been seeking and finding the relics, right? How have they been able to do that?"

Connor dragged a hand over his face. "Let me get this straight. You're shifters from different packs. Shadow Pack or whatever you just called it is the only pack that can access this upside down."

Kael snorted. "Just wait 'till you see the demigorgons."

Callista smacked his arm. "Yes. Lana is Shadow Pack, so she can bring others here."

"Though apparently, I can't take them out," Lana muttered. She lifted her chin, the wheels in her head turning.

Connor paced. "And these alphas you're talking about, they have a relic that lets them do invisibility shit."

"Mmhmm." Destin nodded. "And wind shit."

"Exactly. But they know your magic wolf selves." Connor stopped next to my bedpost. I looked between him and Destin. I couldn't take this conversation seriously. But the summary was surprisingly helpful.

We like him. My wolf settled her head on her paws.

I ignored her and stepped forward. "They don't know me. I've never been up here before, and I've never met the alphas."

"No." Connor's voice was sharp.

My eyes widened. "No, what?"

Connor's eyes bore into me, his jaw flexing. "No."

I scoffed. "Okay, Dad."

Connor flinched, and I regretted my word choice immediately. He looked away, his expression hard. "I don't know anything about this world, but in mine, we don't send teammates into an unknown situation alone."

I exhaled. "Well, there's nobody else here who can do it."

"I'll go." Gabriel stepped forward. "The alpha's have seen me, but I did not reveal my wolf. I can stay out of sight."

Connor gritted his teeth, but Lana nodded too fast for him to protest. Gabriel strode toward me and reached for my hand. My heart leaped into my throat. I'd volunteered, but it hadn't computed that I'd be leaving instantly. And what would we find on the other side? Hopefully more than an abandoned handbag.

Connor's eyes were dark as Gabriel turned to me. "Ready?"

I wet my lips and nodded. He stepped forward, pulling me

with him, then stopped, blinking. I swallowed hard, dread curling in my gut. "What is it?"

Gabriel turned to Lana. She nodded. "That's what it felt like. When I tried to take him out." She pointed at Connor.

My palms started to sweat. "So . . . we're all stuck here?" I thought it had been only Connor, that it was because he was human. But if none of us could get out?

"What if it's us?" Connor watched me, his eyes dark.

My pulse picked up speed. "I'm not following."

His throat worked. "You were the person I touched when I entered, and now neither of us can leave."

I shook my head. "Someone of Shadow Pack blood—"

"Yeah, I know, but what if it has to be both of us?" Connor glanced at the others. "Unless someone has a better idea? I didn't meet the alphas, and I don't have a wolf. Though I did have a girlfriend once who—"

"Oh my hell, seriously?" I held out my other hand.

Connor raised an eyebrow. "You're going to let me try it?"

Kael coughed. "Title of your sex tape."

I glared at both of them. "My sister might be dead, a fire is consuming half of British Columbia, we're both stuck in the Shadow Realm, and you're making sex tape jokes?"

Kael looked pointedly at his one full arm and the other that was only a stub above the elbow. "Nothing's too depressing for a sex tape joke." Callista conveniently turned her head away from both of us.

I didn't know Kael well enough to make any sort of statement after that, so instead, I gave Connor a look and nodded at my hand. "This isn't going to hold itself." I heard it before the last word left my lips, but the damage was already done.

CHAPTER

EIGHTEEN

The world shattered around me. One second, I was standing in the Shadow Realm, the next, reality slammed into me like a brick wall.

The shadowy veil tore apart, dissolving like paper in a storm. Bright, artificial fluorescent light stabbed at my retinas. Harsh. Glaring.

A hallway stretched before us, and the hum of voices drifted from behind closed doors. The air reeked of disinfectant, but underneath that, something else—sweet and metallic. Blood. I scanned the floor, looking for it, but it was clean. How was the scent that strong?

My gut twisted. Where the hell were we? This looked nothing like the woods we'd left behind.

Before I could get my bearings, movement flashed ahead of us. Down the corridor, a group walked toward us.

Shit.

I grabbed Mia's wrist and pulled her into the nearest room —a tiny, cramped supply closet. Not ideal, but better than nothing.

The door swung shut, and darkness swallowed us. Shelves pressed in from behind me, crammed with supplies. I had to lean against Mia and hold perfectly still not to rattle anything. It took a moment, but my eyes adjusted to the dim glow seeping under the door.

Mia's breath hitched, her back against the wall, her chest rising and falling fast. I was too aware of her. The warmth of her body. The faint tremor in her muscles.

The fact that I had her pinned underneath me. Again.

She let out a sharp exhale. "Great plan. We can see so much from in here."

"Got a better idea?" My voice came out rougher than I intended.

Mia scowled. "Yeah. Maybe not barreling into a—"

Before she could finish, we both froze. Footsteps. Heavy. Deliberate. Right outside.

Mia's fingers tightened around mine, and I dropped my forehead to the wall beside her, trying to slow my heart rate. It was fine. We'd randomly appeared in a strange building we knew nothing about, teeming with people who were quite possibly connected to dangerous magical wolves. You know, since they were existing in the center of a damn wildfire.

None of this was on my bingo card for winter break.

Mia's heartbeat was wild. Faster than a rabbit's. I could feel it everywhere. And that? That was a problem. Because I wasn't supposed to be able to feel her like this.

I wasn't supposed to be able to track her pulse like a second heartbeat inside my own chest, feel the heat radiating off her like something molten, something barely contained.

It was messing with my head. I hadn't been with a woman in a long time. Not since I found out the woman I married—the woman I built a life around, the woman who looked me in the eye and promised me forever—had been sleeping with someone else.

And the worst part? I still didn't know why. I still didn't know what I did wrong.

I'd given her everything I could. Worked my ass off. Made sure she and Elle had whatever they needed. I thought I was a good husband.

Turns out? I was wrong. That night broke something in me, and in the following months, I told myself I'd never feel that way again.

I was done being weak. I was done being blindsided. So I changed.

I became a firefighter because I wanted to burn away the man I used to be, the one who trusted too easily, the one who never saw it coming. But standing here next to Mia, I realized I still knew shit nothing about women.

Her pulse hammered, her breath quick and shallow.

"It's fine. We're fine," I murmured in her ear, willing her to calm down. A voice sounded in the room past the door, then floated as the footsteps retreated.

Mia sagged against the wall, her fingers relaxing.

I drew in a greedy breath. "So. That was fun."

"Mm. Suffocating in a broom closet. My favorite." She ducked out from under my arm and reached for the door.

"What the hell are you doing?"

She turned her head. "Leaving so I can breathe."

"Give it a second."

Mia hesitated, her hand still on the doorknob, her shoulders tense. "I think I know the direction of where that handbag is. I'm going to try and find it."

I frowned. "Okay. Thanks for the heads up?" Of course we were looking for the handbag. That was the whole reason we came, wasn't it?

"If you want to wait here—"

"Are you kidding me?" I snapped and stepped forward until our bodies were nearly flush. "You heard what I said. Nobody goes in alone."

Mia's hand twitched on the handle. She wanted to argue, I could feel it. My heart hammered against my ribs. Something had happened when she was lying in my bed. When we heard that growl in the underbrush.

I couldn't explain it, but it felt like I could read her. Like her emotions were so transparent, I could see them coming before they hit.

She turned the knob. "If you get caught, I'm shifting and leaving your human ass behind."

I lowered my head, reveling in the way her breath caught. "But what if I get cold?"

Mia made a sound in her throat, then cracked the door just enough to peek through the gap. I grinned. She deserved that after calling me the D-word. I was technically a dad, but I wasn't old enough to be her dad. That was a significant point.

Satisfied that the coast was clear, Mia slid out into the hall. I followed close behind, my senses on high alert. I wasn't exactly built for stealth, but years of fire rescues had taught me how to move fast.

I followed Mia out into the hall, and when she stopped short, nearly plowed over her.

She turned, her eyes flicking to a door at the end of the hall. "That way."

Thankfully, there were no other voices drifting toward us, but I still hated feeling exposed. Anyone could open a door and find us there. Would it matter? Would they recognize that we were outsiders?

There was nothing along the interior walls that gave any indication of what this place was. A hotel? A wellness center?

That would be on the nose. If even shifter alphas chose a bougie-ass location to hold their seance.

Finally, we reached the door Mia had been leading us toward. It took everything in me not to pull her out of the way and insist I go into the room first, but I held my tongue as she pushed it open slowly, peering inside.

From where I stood, I could just make out the small room beyond. And there, sitting on the floor by the bed, was the handbag.

Mia let out a sharp breath, relief and something else—something deeper—crossing her face. But before I could follow her inside, she froze.

I followed her gaze, my stomach clenching.

There, lying in the bed, curled up beneath the sheets...

Mia's entire body locked up. I didn't have to ask. I already knew.

Her sister. Erin.

NINETEEN

MIA

I rushed forward, not able to believe what I was seeing. It was her. My sister. I had to touch her, make sure she was real.

But before I could get close enough, my wolf slammed into me like a rogue wave. The force of it nearly doubled me over, my stomach clenching, heat surging through my limbs like fire.

Connor grabbed my arm. "Mia—"

I stumbled back. My wolf was howling, thrashing, snapping her teeth. Something was wrong. Something was very, very wrong.

I swallowed, nodding toward the exit. "We need to go. Now."

Connor didn't argue.

We slipped out of the room and through the exit at the end

of the hall. My wolf wasn't explaining, but I'd learned to trust her over the years. She must've sensed something I didn't. But I couldn't just walk away.

Circling around the building, I found Erin's window easily. The curtains were pulled mostly closed, but there was a small gap where I could see her curled up under the covers.

She looked so small. Vulnerable. I pressed my hand against the window frame and tested the lock. It shifted just enough. Perfect.

Connor crouched beside me, his breath warm against my shoulder. "You sure about this?"

I ignored him and slid the window open an inch. Enough to whisper her name, wake her up without drawing attention and without making my wolf lose her ever-loving-mind. "Erin—"

A light flicked on.

I yanked back, pressing myself against the wall. Connor followed, tucking into the shadows, his body half-covering mine as we flattened against the building.

Footsteps.

My wolf bristled, her hackles rising, ears pinned flat against her skull. Whoever that was—they weren't safe. I risked a glance into the window. With the light on and the sun already set, I doubted they'd be able to see past the pane.

The man who entered was tall and broad-shouldered, his presence commanding, suffocating. Dark hair, piercing blue eyes, and a cruel, knowing smile that sent a violent shiver down my spine.

His magic filled the space like a storm cloud, dark and pulsing, a silent predator slinking through the air. My wolf let out a low, guttural snarl in my mind, clawing at the surface.

I held my breath as soon as I saw it. An amulet. Hanging around his neck. Connor slipped a hand around me, sheltering me with his arm and shoulder. I didn't dare move. The truth was, even though it was ridiculous that he thought I needed protection . . . it was also oddly comforting. The males in my pack were protective, but this felt different. Personal.

Erin stirred. She blinked blearily, her golden-brown eyes sharpening with recognition. "James. You look like hell."

The man huffed out a laugh. "I feel like it too."

Erin sat up, rubbing a hand down her face. Her hair was dark like mine but cut shorter, the ends brushing her shoulders in waves. She was leaner than I remembered, her cheekbones sharper, but she still had the same stubborn set to her jaw.

She studied him, frowning. "You've been wearing it too long."

James's fingers drifted to the amulet resting against his chest.

He was tired. I could see it in the slight drag of his movements, the way his shoulders dipped before he rolled them back.

"Don't mother me, Erin," he murmured. "It's fine."

She didn't look convinced. "You have to take a break from it."

James rubbed the bridge of his nose. "I know."

Erin tilted her head. "Does that make you nervous?"

James grinned, flashing white teeth. "Not at all. It'll be behind the wards. Safe."

I sucked in a sharp breath, my mind whirling. Wards? *They left it alone?*

Connor's fingers brushed my arm, a silent question. I didn't answer. My gaze flicked back to Erin. She shifted slightly, her hand moving under the pillow. A second later, I caught a glimpse of something tucked beneath it. A book. She was hiding it from him.

Hope bloomed in my chest.

James exhaled and stood. "Get some sleep, Erin." And then he turned, heading for the door.

I didn't hesitate. I grabbed Connor's wrist and yanked him back toward the shadows. James was leaving. And we were going to follow him.

"What are wards?" Connor whispered as we jogged back around the building.

"Magic. Protections." I stayed low, but Connor crouched down to keep his head below the bushes.

"That's the relic, isn't it?"

I nodded. It had to be. Why else would he be protecting it?

James exited through the same door we'd just passed through. Holy shit. No wonder my wolf had been losing it. She must have sensed him coming from another part of the building.

He moved with purpose, his boots near-silent against the ground as he made his way toward the forest edge. Connor and I stayed back, matching his movements, keeping low.

Connor muttered something under his breath, but I didn't hear it. Because James was stopping. Right at the edge of a clearing.

My breath hitched. Magic curled through the air, thick and old.

James lifted the amulet from around his neck, holding it in his palm. For a moment, he just stood there, staring at it. His shoulders tightened, and then, with a sigh, he lifted his other hand, tracing a symbol in the air.

The air shimmered, rippling like disturbed water. James stepped forward—and vanished.

Connor swore under his breath. "He just—"

I nodded, pulse pounding. Magic hummed before us, and I

pulled Connor back behind the shrubbery. I had no idea where James had gone, and I didn't want to discover he was wandering around invisible like Kael had talked about.

We had to find out where he'd gone—where he was hiding the amulet. And I had an idea of exactly where we might be able to get some inside information.

TWENTY

CONNOR

Something was wrong with me. I'd spent most of my adult life running into danger, but I had never—never—felt like this before. Like my body was tuned to another person's frequency, like every single instinct in me knew exactly where she was, what she was feeling, like my damn heartbeat wouldn't steady unless I knew she was safe.

It wasn't normal. And it sure as hell wasn't rational. But what about this situation was?

I didn't ask questions, just jogged next to Mia until we were back, staring at Erin's window. We crouched close enough to see through the slot, the darkness thick around us.

The light was off now, but Mia was waiting. I didn't need to know why, but I could only stand the silence for so long. The window was open, so even though we were more than a few paces away, I leaned in close. "Do you think he went to the Shadow Realm?"

Mia drew a breath and exhaled, then reached for my shoulder to stabilize herself as she moved her mouth next to my ear. "No idea." She kept her cheek pressed against mine.

I swallowed hard. "Do you think Lana and the others can see us here?"

She pulled back, her expression questioning. She blinked, then pointed her finger and started drawing something in the air in front of her. I didn't even pretend to be able to read it.

She finished her finger painting, then restarted, leaning close again. "Not sure if this will make any sense," she murmured.

"Crystal clear for me, so . . . "

Mia blew out a breath that almost sounded like a laugh. When she finished the second time, she dropped her hand, resting it on my arm. "I'm waiting for her to fall asleep."

I nodded. Again, didn't make sense, but I kept my mouth shut. I didn't see how a sleeping sister could give us any information, but I'd already asked two stupid questions.

Mia pulled back, and the night air rushed in against my neck. I instantly wanted to pull her back, but clenched my fists instead. I couldn't stop thinking about what had happened in the Shadow Realm. How Mia had lit up, how she'd arched against me and dragged her lips over my skin.

Questions sat on the tip of my tongue, but before I could make sense of them, Mia was creeping toward the window. I followed and held my breath when she reached up to pull the window open further.

It stuck, and Mia froze. She released her grip and wrung out her hands, then reached up and tried again.

I wanted to reach up and help, but didn't want to piss her off again. I was trying to remember that she had power I couldn't see, but it wasn't computing. I definitely didn't see her as a kid anymore, not by a long shot. But she still seemed so delicate. Fragile.

Mia blew out a breath, her eyes flashing. She turned to me and pulled me to her by my shirt. "It's stuck," she whispered.

I grinned, then quickly sobered. "Breaking and entering wasn't part of my job description."

Mia pulled back and arched a brow. "Then maybe you should've stayed in your fire truck," she mouthed.

Smart-ass.

I reached into my pocket and pulled out my pocket knife. Thankfully, that had moved inter-dimensionally no problem. I put my hands on her waist and moved her to my other side, then flicked the knife open. I reached up and slid the blade between the frame, wiggling it carefully.

It felt so damn good to be useful.

It took a second, but the window gave a soft crack. Success. I shot her a smug look before carefully lifting it open an inch, then another. Then I stepped back and kneeled, motioning for her to use my thigh as a step stool.

She pursed her lips, then full-on bypassed me and hoisted herself up silently, slipping into the room like a shadow. Uh, okay. Maybe I was the one who needed a boost. Or maybe she didn't want me—

Mia's head poked out, and she offered her hand. I waved her off. With adrenaline coursing through my veins, I pulled myself up, the frame biting into my palms. When I had enough leverage, I slid one forearm in, giving myself enough strength to push up to my waist. I slung my leg in and, much less gracefully, flipped through, landing on the floor with a dull thud.

I froze, hoping I hadn't given us away. When I didn't hear movement, I turned.

Mia crept forward and knelt beside the bed. She held there

a moment, watching. I stayed put, not wanting to ruin the moment. Then she turned and mouthed, "I have to touch her."

She held up a hand, and something cold rolled down my spine. "Mia—"

She gave me a look that said, "Trust me," and I bit off the end of that retort. But as Mia brushed her sister's sleeve up her arm and lay her hand on her skin, that trust shattered.

Mia's body arched violently, her breath leaving in a sharp, strangled sound.

"Shit—Mia!" I lunged for her, catching her before her head slammed against the bedpost. But then—

I felt it.

A pull. Not like the cell-splitting yank I'd felt when I followed Mia into the Shadow Realm, but an instant plummet. Like diving off the side of a cliff.

And then I was no longer in Erin's room. I was moving through something unseen, intangible. My vision twisted and blurred, shifting, reshaping. When I landed, I wasn't me anymore. I was looking through someone else's eyes.

Pain ripped through me. Loneliness. I was a rogue—I didn't even know what that word meant, but it stuck to me like a used dryer sheet. I moved from place to place and heard rumors. Wolves were missing, friends were afraid.

Then the vision twisted, and I was someone new. I was—

Holy shit. I was looking at . . . myself. A younger version of me. Ten years ago. I knew because that was when I was still shaving every day.

I no longer felt alone. I was curious. I wanted to impress *me*.

I almost choked when my sight adjusted, and there was Elle. My daughter when she was young. Which meant . . . I was Mia. They were crafting at the kitchen table.

Another twist. I was looking through the same eyes, this

time sitting across from Mia's mother and father. And Erin. She sat next to me, laughing at something I'd said.

Then a knock on the door. Mia's father got up, setting his napkin next to his plate. He walked to the door and opened it.

Fear coursed through me in a jolt. Nathan Black. He walked into the house with two other men I didn't recognize.

Then it was all pain. White-hot, searing pain.

I was in Mia's body, trapped as she watched Nathan Black rip her mother's shirt from her back, exposing skin to the cold night air.

I felt the lash, and everything inside me went ice cold. Mia's mother barely flinched. The first time. Then the rage and horror made my vision blur.

Nathan's voice rang out: "You exposed us."

A growl ripped from my throat. I wanted to kill him.

And then I was running through the woods. Alone. Afraid. Looking for Destin. But I couldn't find him.

Wolves were disappearing. Someone—a male rogue wolf —had told me to go home.

But I wouldn't. I couldn't. Not after what Nathan Black had done to my mother.

And then—

The man with the amulet. James.

He found me and promised me vengeance. Told me he'd give me Nathan Black's head.

I reached for the amulet. Felt the darkness in it. The pull. It should have scared me. But it didn't. It felt like power. Like the strength I had always wanted, had always needed.

My head suddenly felt thick. Pressure swelled at the edge of the memory, someone's will straining against the tide.

No, Mia's voice whispered, her presence coiling against mine, desperate and fierce. *Don't take it. Don't let him pull you in.*

I tried. Tried to resist, tried to pull my hand back. But James was smiling. Smiling like he already knew how this would end. Like I had already been his from the start.

I wrapped my fingers around the amulet, and everything went black.

When the darkness lifted, James walked beside me. The amulet gleamed at his throat, pulsing with a slow, steady heartbeat. We moved between buildings through what looked like a command center. Like the one I built out of tents and trailers with my team.

Men and women moved through the space with purpose, not like survivors but like soldiers. James walked through the main structure, stepping inside a large open hall where two other men waited.

They turned when we entered. One was wiry, the other massive, towering over the first with a scowl on his face. James spoke to them and motioned to me, but I couldn't understand what they were saying. I opened my mouth, but nothing coherent came out.

James turned back to me, his lips curling into something cold. "You've been helpful, Erin. But we both know you're not ready." His hand shot forward, fingers gripping my throat.

I didn't flinch. Didn't struggle. But my wolf screamed inside me. I gasped at the feel of it, the all-consuming presence.

"Do what I ask, and your pack will survive," James murmured. "Fail me, and they will be erased." His grip tightened. My lungs burned. And then he smiled. "As long as you do your job, I don't care what happens to them. But if you cross me?" He tilted his head. "I'll make sure you watch as every single one of them burns."

He let go. I collapsed to my knees, gasping. The men watched without expression. James stepped back and reached for the amulet. I barely lifted my head as he walked toward the far end of the hall.

James lifted his hand, traced something in the air. A pulse of magic rippled outward, revealing a barrier hidden inside the structure. A warded cage. And without hesitation, he placed the amulet inside.

And then I was falling again.

The second I hit the ground, I jolted back to reality. I dragged in a breath, my vision clearing. I was in Erin's bedroom, but something was wrong. I lifted my head. Mia was on her knees, breathing hard, her body shaking.

Before I could reach for her, fur exploded from her skin. She transformed violently in front of my eyes. Snarling, bristling, her golden eyes burning with rage.

My mind was wiped clean. I couldn't think—couldn't process what I'd just seen. Her growl vibrated through my ribs, my instincts screaming at me to run.

But I couldn't. Mia was in there, and after what I'd just seen, I had no idea what her mental state was. "Hey," I said carefully, keeping my hands open, my voice even. "Mia, you're—"

She snapped her teeth, her ears pinned back, muscles coiled like she was ready to pounce.

My throat went dry. "Mia," I tried again, my heart hammering. "It's me. Connor."

Her body coiled, but just as her head lowered and her hackles rose, her attention shifted.

I spun around to find the man with the amulet. James. Standing in the doorway.

CHAPTER

TWENTY-ONE

MIA

My wolf wanted blood. She didn't especially care whose. The rage burned through me like wildfire, clawing at my insides, twisting, demanding an outlet.

My vision still swam with the images from Erin's memories, burned into me like fresh wounds. I had felt everything.

My mother's pain.

My sister's fear.

My own failure.

And James. That bastard. He'd lured my sister in, promised her vengeance, twisting her until she thought she had no other choice. I had felt Erin's anger, her desperation, the way the amulet had coiled around her like chains she didn't even know she was wearing.

I wanted to rip him apart. I couldn't breathe, couldn't find my way to the surface as my wolf lowered her head and snarled.

A man stood right there. The sharp scent of his sweat, his pulse hammering in his throat, the deep rise and fall of his chest.

He was prey. Human.

No! I cried out. This wasn't right. He wasn't prey. He was something else. Something my wolf recognized, and that only made her more dangerous.

My wolf growled, low and rough in my mind. *He was there. He let it happen.*

Connor. My vision cleared enough that I could make out his face.

We like him, remember? I threw out in desperation, but she was seeing red. I bared my teeth, claws digging into the wood beneath me, my body coiled tight, ready to strike.

He tensed, hands up, open-palmed.

I had to do something, but my wolf was in control now, and she wasn't listening. Breathe. I forced her to drag in his scent. *It's Connor, not Nathan or James!*

I forced the image of him curling over us in the bed, of him pulling us to him outside the window. My shoulders relaxed a fraction when movement caught my eye.

Someone walked in the room with a laugh. The sound of his voice sent a sickening chill down my spine. I growled in warning as he stepped closer.

James. Tall. Broad. Sharp-edged and cruel. The amulet around his neck pulsed with an unnatural glow.

He smirked, watching me with that same amusement like I was nothing but a feral little showpiece for his entertainment. And then his power slammed into me. A crushing, invisible weight forced my body to the ground, pinning my limbs and pressing my chest against the floor.

Connor grunted beside me, his body folding under the pressure.

I snarled, fighting it, but I couldn't move—could barely breathe.

James crouched in front of me, tilting his head. "Well, well. Look what the fire dragged in."

I let out a low, guttural growl, my muscles shaking with the effort to move.

James ran a hand over the amulet, his fingers tapping lazily against its surface. Enjoying this. "Where are the others?" he asked.

I bared my teeth, my canines glistening. I wasn't telling him shit. I tried to move, tried to shift forward, but his magic pressed tighter, suffocating.

He sighed, sounding bored. "Tsk, tsk, little wolf. You still think you have control here."

And then he squeezed his fist, and the command hit like a wrecking ball. Pain tore through me, twisting my limbs, forcing my bones to snap and bend.

I shifted back against my will, gasping as my human body returned. I lay on the floor naked. Exposed. It was all I could do to curl inward, covering myself the best I could. Every nerve screamed.

James just grinned, dragging his gaze over me.

Disgust coiled in my stomach, and rage swallowed it whole. I wanted to gut him. I wanted to tear his face from his skull.

Connor made a low sound of fury, his body still trembling under the weight of the magic.

James turned his gaze to him, lips curling. "Oh, what's this?" he taunted. "You care about her?"

Connor said nothing, but his jaw locked so tight I thought it might break.

James leaned in, voice dropping to something colder, deadlier. "You're weak," he said. "I can't even feel your wolf. Pathetic. She'll break you before this is over."

Connor's nostrils flared, his breath shuddering. He was barely holding it together, and by his expression, James knew it.

But then his smile vanished. He reached out and grabbed me, his fingers biting into my arm, jerking me close. "Do you know what I do to traitors?" he murmured.

I didn't answer. The word traitor set my teeth on edge. I wasn't betraying anyone. I was here to fight for my family, for my pack.

My mind reeled with everything I'd seen. James was the reason for the missing wolves, for Kael coming after Callista, and for who knew what else. I'd heard bits and pieces in Kitimat about the northern alphas, but now I had a face to put to the horror.

James' grip tightened. "I suppose your sister could tell you," he mused. "She's been watching for quite some time."

My stomach turned to stone. He was using Erin. Using her against me. Against herself.

I tried to push up from the floor, but before I could even get close, he threw me backward like I was nothing.

Connor roared, straining against the magic, his eyes wild, furious.

James just sighed. "Perhaps you need some time to think about it. He snapped his fingers, and the next thing I knew, I was in darkness.

A door slammed shut, and I could finally move. I reached for the handle, and a sharp pulse of energy rolled through the air, thick and heavy, sinking into my skin like burning tar. I gasped, my body seizing, shrinking inward.

Then, Connor's hands were on me. He tried to pull me

back, but I reached out, pressing my palm against the wood. A shockwave exploded outward, throwing me across the small space. I hit the wall with a choked sound, my limbs tangled.

Connor was on me in a second, hands grabbing my arms, steadying me.

His hands stilled as I jerked away, trying to cover myself. "I'm sorry, I—"

"No. No, I didn't mean—" his sentence stopped short at a sharp knock on the door.

"Thanks for putting on a fantastic show." James laughed, and then his footsteps retreated.

I swallowed, my throat thick and my body aching from being ripped from my wolf. "Erin?" I cried out, but there was no answer.

"What the hell did he mean by that?" Connor panted, rage rolling off him in waves.

A fantastic show. My stomach dropped. "I think he just answered your question."

"Which one?"

I blew out a ragged breath. "Everyone in the Shadow Realm can definitely see us."

Connor

My eyes adjusted to the slivers of light pushing around the edges of the closet door, and my gaze landed on Mia. My chest had been caving in on itself since I saw her shift, but now I was breaking.

I'd seen it, witnessed what happened to her mother, and it was my fault. I'd gone looking for Nathan Black. I'd told him that someone saw her there at the ambulance—saw her with Elle.

The pain I had caused Mia and her family—no wonder she'd kept her secrets. Why she hadn't trusted me or anyone else in Kitimat and Black Lake.

Her words slammed back into me. *I didn't know what it was like.*

Silently, I peeled off my shirt. The air was thick with the remnants of dark magic, the taste of it metallic on my tongue, but none of it mattered. Not when she was sitting there, exposed and shaking, her breath uneven.

"Here," I murmured, draping the fabric over her shoulders.

She flinched at the touch but didn't refuse. Her hands closed around the edges of the fabric. I couldn't see much more than her eyes, lips, and her silhouette, but still, I turned away, forcing myself to focus on the dark space around us. The closet was cramped, filled with forgotten clothes, musty fabric, and the faint scent of dust. I ran my hands blindly along the shelves, searching.

Nothing.

Then my fingers caught on something soft. I tugged it down—the fabric felt long, two separate pieces. Pants? Leggings? They weren't much, but they were something. I turned back to her, offering them.

She hesitated before snatching them from my hands, shifting awkwardly as she slid them on beneath the oversized shirt. I forced myself to look away again, keeping my eyes on the floor, on the door, anywhere but at her.

When she was done, she exhaled sharply. "These are probably Erin's."

It wasn't a question. I nodded anyway and turned back to face her.

She let out a shaky breath, fingers curling into the material of my shirt. "Why are you looking at me like that?"

I stepped closer and took her hands in mine, my grip steady, warm, grounding. She stiffened, but she didn't pull away. I took a slow breath and dropped to my knees in front of her.

Mia tensed, her brows furrowing. "Connor—"

"It was my fault." My voice came out rough, edged with something raw. "I wasn't there to help you. I wasn't—" I swallowed, shaking my head. "I was only trying to find who healed

Elle." She stiffened, and I squeezed her hands. "I wanted to thank them," I admitted, my voice hoarse. "That's all. That's the only reason I was there, the only reason I talked to him. I didn't know. I just—I just wanted to say thank you."

Mia's eyes were dark, unreadable. Her lips parted, but no sound came. Her throat bobbed, and her fingers trembled in my grip.

The words spilled out of me. "I became a firefighter because I had to do something. I had to save someone. Anyone. Because I couldn't save her. I couldn't save anything—not my daughter, my marriage. I was so weak." I pulled her closer, pressing my face against her stomach, tears spilling from my eyes and soaking my own damn shirt.

I still held her hands, my grip tightening as if letting go would mean losing something I didn't even know I needed until now.

I'd been fighting so long on my own. Fighting for what? To prove myself? And still I stood there, useless.

Mia was silent, her breath steady but slow, as if she were sorting through the weight of my words. My confession still hung between us, raw and aching, but I wasn't done. I couldn't be done. Not until she knew—until she understood.

"I didn't know," I whispered. "I didn't know what they did to you. To your mother. To Erin. I thought—I thought I was doing the right thing, just asking questions. But when your father told me to stop, I—I didn't listen." Guilt clawed at my middle.

Mia exhaled, long and slow. She pulled one of her hands free and, to my surprise, ran her fingers through my hair, threading through the strands. I closed my eyes, letting it ground me, letting the warmth of her fingers quiet the riot inside my chest.

"Connor." Her voice was soft.

I lifted my head from where I'd been bowing in front of her, looking up at her as if she held all the answers. Maybe she did. Maybe she always had. I wasn't sure I deserved to be kneeling at her feet.

I thought of James forcing her to the ground. Tearing her from her wolf. "He hurt you. I wasn't strong enough. I couldn't stop him—"

"Shh." Mia dragged her fingers against my scalp. She didn't pull away. Instead, she cupped the back of my head, holding me to her like I was something worth keeping, worth protecting. The touch only unraveled me further.

I pulled her wrist to my lips. I couldn't stop myself, couldn't think of another way to show her my remorse. To show her how every man in the damn world should have treated her and the other women in her family, in her pack. She needed to hear it, but more than that, she needed to feel it.

I kissed her fluttering pulse, then kissed up the inside of her arm, the bend of her elbow. Higher until I stood, my lips pressing against her cheek, her jaw, her temple—anywhere I could reach. I wasn't thinking, just moving, feeling, giving into the overwhelming rush of emotions clawing through my chest.

I needed to make this right.

I needed to protect her.

It was a visceral, primal need.

And then she kissed me back, her fingers tightening in my hair, her breath hot against my skin. It was desperate, hurried. Apologies. Forgiveness.

I slid my hands to her waist, pulling her closer, feeling the shape of her body against mine. Every inch of her, every second, was a craving, an addiction unlocked.

The intensity of it rocked me to my core.

I had kissed women before. I had held them, touched them,

felt them against me. But never like this. Never with this heat, this desperation, this all-consuming need.

Mia pressed against me, her lips parting, her breath mingling with mine. I could taste her, feel her, but it still wasn't enough.

I needed her. Not in a sweet, soft, easy kind of way. No, this was the kind of need that hurt, that twisted deep inside your ribs and refused to let go.

Because I saw her.

I saw her strength, her unwavering loyalty to her sister, to her pack. She was strong. She was everything I wasn't.

I pulled back, my breathing ragged, my forehead pressing against hers. "I'm sorry," I rasped. "I didn't—"

She silenced me by pulling me close, bending me closer, guiding my head against her chest, holding me there.

I wrapped my arms around her waist and let myself be held. I was flayed open, completely exposed. And she wasn't pushing me away.

We stayed like that for a while, breathing together. It took longer than I would've expected for the shame and embarrassment to rush in. My walls slowly started to rise, heat flashing through me.

"Don't," she murmured. My breathing quickened. "You're not weak."

I straightened, pulling my head from her chest and standing at my full height. I dropped my hands from her hips. "Well, the shifter with the necklace seems to disagree." I made a damn joke. Because that's what I did—what I always did.

Mia grabbed my hips and slammed me against her. "What did you say?" Her eyes flashed.

I swallowed. "He said I was weak—"

"No, what did he say exactly?" Mia's grip tightened.

I scanned my memory. "He said he couldn't feel my wolf." I

refrained from commenting on how his hands weren't even close to my pants.

Mia's breathing quickened. "Did you touch the door?"

I frowned and shook my head. "Wasn't tempting. I saw what it did to you."

She nodded, eyes sharp. "Right. But I'm a shifter."

"Yes . . . and?"

"James. He assumed you're one of us." She released me. "Whatever magic he wove, it worked to keep me out."

"But I'm not a shifter." I turned, my eyes locked on the handle. I took a step and reached out. It was either going to turn or I was going to land on my ass.

CHAPTER
TWENTY-THREE

Connor's fingers curled around the door handle. I watched, my breath held tight in my chest, expecting to see him shocked back, thrown to the floor just like I had been. But nothing happened.

The door opened smoothly, silently. Like the magic had never been there at all. I blinked, my brain stuttering over the impossibility of it.

Connor turned back to me, his hazel eyes widening. "Holy shit."

I didn't move. Couldn't. My thoughts were still tangled in what had just happened between us.

His hands in my hair. His lips against my skin. The way he had dropped to his knees in front of me, so raw, so vulnerable, so . . . human. I had never seen a man, especially one like Connor, do anything like that before.

There was a swoop in my belly at the memory of him tipping his chin, looking up at me shirtless with his hands wrapped around my waist. I wasn't angry with him. How could I be?

He didn't understand, and when he'd seen everything, he hadn't fought against it. He didn't for a second pretend he'd been right. It was the last thing I'd expected.

My wolf was still restless, prowling, agitated. She should have been pushing me away from him, but instead, she wanted him closer. *Not possible,* I reminded her, pressing my nails into my palms.

Wolves didn't bond with humans. And even if they did, it always ended badly.

We'd all heard the stories. Some wolves had tried to take a human mate, tried to deny their instincts, tried to bend nature to something it was never meant to be. It never worked.

A wolf's magic was woven into their blood, into their bones. A bond had to be reciprocated, recognized. If it wasn't, it shattered them, drained them. Made them . . . *less.*

The ones who fought the bond and forced it anyway? Most of them had lost their ability to shift. Some had gone mad.

Connor crossed the threshold and stepped into the room, glancing around. "They're gone."

I peered through the open door, my heart picking up speed, but he was right. The room was empty. Relief surged through me, and I moved to step out after him, hopeful that maybe—

Agony.

The second my foot crossed the threshold, I was slammed backward, my spine colliding with the wall. A white-hot wave of magic coiled tight around my chest, squeezing, pressing, refusing to let me pass. I gasped, my vision going white.

"Mia!" Connor was immediately back in the closet, hands on my shoulders, checking me over. "What happened?"

I sucked in air, heart racing, wolf snarling. "It seems I can't leave."

Connor's brows pulled together. He reached for my wrist, thumb rubbing slow circles against my pulse point. "But the door—"

"It's still holding me." My breath was ragged, frustration bleeding into every word. "James' magic—whatever it is—it won't let me pass."

Connor's grip tightened. "Then I'm not going anywhere."

I shook my head. "You have to."

Connor stiffened. "Mia, I'm not leaving you in here."

"I know where the wards are." I lifted my chin, swallowing against the pain of the words. "I saw them in Erin's vision."

Connor's jaw clenched. He nodded once. "I saw it, too."

I pushed up to sit straight. "You have to find the hall—"

"Mia, this is crazy. I know nothing about this world. What if I can't find it? Or what if I don't come back?"

"You will."

"*Mia.*"

My name was a plea, and in his eyes . . .

I stiffened and pulled back, then forced myself up off the floor. I scanned the closet now that I could see more than a few inches in front of my face. I needed to shut this down. I had to. I couldn't allow him to keep looking at me that way—to think that something between us was possible.

My throat thickened as I snatched a shirt off a hanger. The fabric was soft, worn, probably something Erin had left behind. I turned my back to him and yanked his shirt off, replacing it with the navy pullover. "You have to go," I snapped. "Now. If you want any chance of stopping the fire."

He stilled behind me. I waited, but he didn't move. Didn't speak.

My heart was still pounding, my body aching from everything—the vision, the magic, the way Connor had touched me like I was something fragile and precious.

I couldn't afford to feel that way. Not about him. I needed to focus on the problem at hand. My sister was with that monster, and we needed to find the relic.

So I did what I had always done. What I had done when I watched my mother take the punishment from Nathan Black. What I had done when Erin walked away from me, choosing exile.

I pulled up the wall. Buried it all. I was a shifter. He was human. That was the end of it.

My wolf whined, and that pissed me off. How was I the one speaking reason in this situation?

I felt him leave and still waited a full minute before turning. I swallowed hard and pressed my hands against my arms, trying to keep my body from trembling.

"Lana, where the hell are you?" I hissed under my breath. The whole reason they hadn't come in the first place was to keep our presence a secret, but now that was blown wide open. So where were they? Why was I stuck in a damn closet, and Connor was hunting down the amulet?

I sucked in a sharp breath and turned back toward the wall, lifting my hand, tracing more words into the air.

Lana. Destin. Someone. Someone had to see this. I couldn't just sit in this closet, trapped while Connor walked out into the lion's den alone. My magic flickered as I pressed harder, channeling all my frustration, all my desperation into the symbols.

And then there was a sharp, suffocating pull at my middle. The band of magic around my skin tightened. Crushing. I gasped, legs buckling, chest seizing.

My wolf snarled, thrashed, pushed against the magic, but it wouldn't let go. I fell back against the wall, gasping for breath.

If Connor didn't find the wards, if he didn't come back soon—

I wasn't sure if I'd still be here when he did.

CHAPTER

TWENTY-FOUR

Connor

Mia's rejection hit like a blow to the chest. One minute, she was holding me, grounding me, kissing me back with the same desperate need I felt. And the next, she was shutting down, pulling away like a steel trap snapping closed.

I didn't get it. I didn't understand. She had let me in, just for a moment. Let me see her pain, her fear, the weight she carried alone. And I had given her mine in return, laying myself bare in a way I never had before.

And now? She had turned away from me like it had meant nothing. The shame of showing that kind of weakness curled in my gut like a sickness.

But then . . .

She'd said the words. Maybe it wasn't weakness at all.

Because that same weakness James sneered at had let me out of the damn closet.

I hated leaving Mia behind. It went against every instinct I had. But I had to do what I could to find the amulet.

I crept through the hallways, keeping low, keeping to the edges of the walls where the floorboards didn't creak. The building was eerily silent.

James and Erin were gone for now, and I didn't know how long that would last. I exhaled slowly, pushing forward, stepping out into the open night.

The fire still raged in the distance, a steady glow on the horizon. It should have been terrifying, knowing how close we were to a living inferno.

But now I knew.

It wasn't natural.

James had manipulated it. Controlled it.

And somehow, he was keeping this place safe, untouched, standing in the eye of the storm like a damn king.

I moved through the buildings, sticking to the shadows, but the truth was, I didn't know where the hell I was going. In the vision, I'd seen the hall just like Mia had. I had seen its walls, the way it was structured. But none of that told me how to find it.

I crouched behind a stack of wooden crates, scanning the area. The layout here was strategic. Nothing was thrown together. These buildings weren't just random shelters—they had a purpose.

I thought about the command centers I had built on wildfire sites. The largest buildings were always central. The first rule of any operation was keeping the chain of command in place. They wouldn't put something important near the edge of the camp—it would be too vulnerable.

I pressed my fingers against my temple, picturing the

vision again. The building had been deep in the camp, past a row of smaller buildings.

I needed height. A vantage point.

My gaze landed on a supply shed with a narrow overhang. Not great, but it would do.

Moving quickly, I darted across the clearing and jumped, catching the lip of the roof. My muscles strained as I pulled myself up, rolling onto my stomach and pressing flat against the surface.

Thankfully the moon was almost full. From here, I could see everything. The pathways between buildings. The movement of people—scattered now, but deliberate.

And there—near the center of the camp—was a structure bigger than the rest.

That had to be it.

I slid back down, landing with a soft grunt, then crept forward. It took a few minutes to make my way over, but I knew I was in the right place when I pulled the door open.

I waited, scanning for movement or sound.

When I heard nothing, I pulled the door a bit wider, only to jump back as a figure appeared in front of me.

Just as I was about to throw myself behind the corner of the building, a hand caught my elbow and yanked me inside.

I reacted instinctively, throwing a punch that landed against something as solid as concrete. "Mother f—"

"Shut it, Chief."

My head snapped up, my jaw dropping open. Kael. His golden eyes burned in the dim light, his grip like steel around my arm. He released me a second later, shaking his head. "You're going to wake the whole house."

I clenched my fists, biting back several responses. Instead, I exhaled sharply and straightened, scanning behind him. "You're here? Are the others—?"

"They're still in the Shadow Realm," he cut in. "They can't see anything here. You know where it is?" I nodded and pointed to the far wall. Kael ran. "I think I can take it."

I crossed the room after him. I saw what James' wards had done to Mia.

"Where's Mia?" Kael pressed his hands against the wall, searching for an opening.

"James warded the—"

"You saw James?" I nodded, but Kael was already talking again. "A little direction?"

I pointed to the location on the wall I remembered, not sure if it was anywhere close.

"So you left Mia."

"I didn't leave her," I growled. "She told me to go."

"Huh. Surprising after that show you two put on."

My eyes flew wide. Oh shit. They could see us. They'd seen every second of that.

"Don't worry, we couldn't hear anything. Callista was pissed. She wanted to hear—"

"Just find the damn necklace."

Kael smirked. "Now I wish I heard—" He stopped mid sentence as a faint shimmer pulsed in the air. Kael's hands brushed over the wall, landing where we'd seen it.

The shimmer rippled, revealing a carved-out alcove in the wall. A cage, exactly as I'd seen in Erin's memory. Inside, the amulet sat pulsing faintly.

Kael exhaled. He hesitated, then extended his hand. "Seems Destin was right."

"Right? About—" The words died on my lips as the air shifted. Wind roared to life, sweeping through the room and slamming into us.

Heat flared, rushing up from the floor, searing through my

skin. Kael's eyes snapped up. And the last thing I saw before flames swallowed us whole was James's smile.

CHAPTER
TWENTY-FIVE

The band around my chest vanished so fast it was like I'd been released from a vice. For a brief, glorious second, I could breathe, and then the rush hit.

Something was wrong. Not just wrong—disastrous. The air changed, the pressure around me shifting like a storm breaking over the horizon. Instinct kicked in before I had time to think.

I tore out of the closet and into the night. Connor. That was my first thought.

Was he safe? Had he made it out? The last time I saw him, he was walking away from me, hurt and confused. Now, I didn't know where he was. If he'd found the amulet. If he was still alive.

I gritted my teeth. The camp was chaos. Smoke curled low over the ground, thick and suffocating, pressing into my lungs. The fire was closer now. Too close.

Where was Erin? My mind spun as my feet pounded against the ground. She was with James, but why? I'd seen her suffering in the vision, the way she had been caught in his trap, but she was by his side. Hiding things from him, but still listening to his lies.

That terrified me more than the fire. Was she under his command? Had he used the amulet on her? I needed to find them.

I cut between the buildings, everything golden in the light from the encroaching flames. I scanned the area, trying to piece together the vision I'd seen in Erin's memories.

The hall. It had been deep in the camp, somewhere central, somewhere protected. But where?

I skidded to a stop, my chest heaving. Think, Mia. I'd seen the open doors in Erin's mind. I spun in a circle, searching, then grunted as something ran headlong into me.

"Mia?"

My heart jolted. "Lana?" I nearly shrieked with relief, but then worry hit me in the chest. She was here which meant—

"Finally," she snapped, grabbing my arm. "We've been looking everywhere for you."

Callista, Gabriel, and Destin were right behind her, all of them tense, breathless. Gabriel's face was set in a hard line, Callista's brows furrowed. Destin looked half-feral, his jaw clenched.

"We don't have time," Callista said. "Kael and Connor are in trouble."

Connor. His name sent a jolt through my chest.

"Where?" I demanded.

Lana pointed ahead. "This way. Run."

I didn't hesitate. I bolted after her, my breath coming fast and shallow. The fire grew, licking hungrily at the edges of the buildings, curling up toward the dark sky.

We slammed through the doors to the hall and found Kael, Connor—both of them on their knees, surrounded by a torrent.

James stood between them, his hands raised, fingers splayed, as if conducting the flames like an orchestra. Fire twisted around them, circling in tight, moving in perfect tandem with James's will.

Kael held the amulet, and Connor—

I clutched my middle. Connor wasn't a wolf. He didn't have the resistance, the healing, the innate survival that came with being a shifter. To Kael, this was painful. To Connor? This was deadly. He was human, and James didn't know. Or maybe he did at this point and didn't care.

"Why didn't you come sooner?" I cried out.

Lana sucked in a breath, forcing the words through clenched teeth. "We had to stay hidden," she rasped. "We couldn't let him sense Kael's blood—not until we knew where the amulet was."

I stumbled, my mind reeling.

Kael's blood?

What was she talking about?

James chuckled, pacing between Connor and Kael as if he owned the battlefield.

"How very clever of you," he mused. "If only you'd thought to keep the Shadow Pack blood back. That was a direct beacon to your arrival."

Lana frowned, confusion flickering over her face, but James was already moving.

He turned his attention fully on Kael. "I should have killed you when I had the chance."

Kael gritted his teeth, his golden eyes blazing.

James smirked. "But this is better, isn't it? A little family reunion."

Holy hell.

Kael? He was James' son?

My wolf snarled inside me, furious, protective, desperate. She didn't care about the lines we had drawn, about the way I had pushed him away before. Right now, there was only one truth.

Connor was mine. And if James thought he could burn him alive, he'd have to go through me first. I searched for some way to get to him, my eyes darting wildly through the wall of fire, and that's when I saw Erin.

She was just standing there. I yelled her name, waving frantically to get her attention through the blaze. She flinched.

She saw me. But she didn't move. Why? What could she possibly have to offer James? Why would he need her enough to put this kind of effort into keeping her?

There had to be something I was missing. There had to be something—

"Mia! Don't! Don't move!"

My head whipped back to Lana.

She was breathing hard, one hand pressed against her thigh where the dagger was still strapped. Her face twisted, her knees buckling beneath her.

And then I felt it, too. The air thickened. A pull so deep it felt like my bones were vibrating.

The power of the relics surged, pressing against my ribs. I gasped, struggling to take in air. I barely had time to process before James twisted his fingers. The fire surged. Kael gasped, his back arching, his muscles locking.

Connor let out a strangled noise, his body trembling from the heat. They were both burning.

A feral snarl cut through the crackling fire. I turned just in time to see Callista lunge. I knew exactly how she felt. She wasn't thinking—wasn't planning. Her only thought was Kael.

She didn't care about the fire, the relics, James' twisted power. She only saw him suffering.

She slammed into the invisible barrier James had woven, but the magic caught her, twisting around her body and throwing her back. She hit the ground hard, spitting blood, but she was already pushing herself back up. "Let him go!"

James barely glanced at her as the amulet pulsed, a second heartbeat in the air. Lana gasped, her body jerking as the dagger began to glow, and suddenly, the fire wasn't just James' weapon.

Lana dragged herself up with Destin at her side. He reached for the dagger, but she pulled it back. "No. They're reaching for each other. I think I can—" Lana flicked her wrist, the flames danced.

James' nostrils flared, and he sent a gust of wind so strong it could break bones. Lana countered, the dagger in her grip absorbing the force, her eyes burning like embers as she charged forward with Destin desperately trying to keep up. The ground trembled beneath us, relics screaming for control.

But Connor was still burning.

I couldn't do this. I couldn't watch him die. I lunged forward, desperate to reach him, to do something, anything—

But I slammed into Lana instead. Her balance broke, her control shattered. The dagger flew from her hands.

I hit the ground, air torn from my lungs, my body twisting as the flames surged back, uncontested.

James smiled, fully in control now. "I gave you a choice," he murmured. He lifted his hand, and Lana screamed.

Wind ripped through the clearing, shredding against her exposed skin. She collapsed, gasping, struggling against the force, her body curling inward.

James' face twisted. "The book!"

Lana choked. "I don't—"

James flicked his wrist, and the wind doubled. Lana's skin split at the pressure, blood dripping onto the dirt. Destin roared, clawing his way forward, but James only tilted his head, amused.

"Where is it?"

Lana didn't answer. She couldn't. She was breaking.

And then, in a split second, everything stopped. The flames vanished. The wind died.

James was no longer facing us. I pushed up from the ground, searching.

My blood froze in my veins. Connor. He stood, his skin raw and blistered with the dagger in his hand, pressed against Kael's throat.

He drew in a ragged breath. "You don't need them. I can tell you where the book is."

TWENTY-SIX

M IA

Connor stood before James, the dagger pressed against Kael's throat, his face set in grim determination. His body trembled from the heat, sweat glistening on his skin, but his voice didn't waver.

"You want the book," he said, staring James down. "I know where it is."

"No!" Callista screamed, her body shaking. "Don't touch his blood!" Tears streamed down her face, and my heart broke for her. I knew her story, the entire pack did. How she'd been cut with the dagger and how the blade wouldn't stop until it took her life. If Connor slipped or pressed too hard, it was a death sentence.

"Connor!" I shouted. "Don't do this!"

His eyes flicked to mine, and everything inside me stilled. Trust me.

James tilted his head, considering him like a cat watching a mouse walk willingly into its claws. "How would you know where this book is?" His voice dripped with amusement. "You fooled me once, human. I won't allow you to fool me again."

Connor's grip on the relic tightened as Kael tried to break free. "You know, honestly, I thought you'd be smarter. I'm a human, and I can see what you can't." James' eyes flared, but Connor didn't give him a chance to respond. "Why do you think she can hold the power of the amulet and you struggle?"

James' eyes flicked to Erin, and the breath whooshed from my lungs. She was pressed against the wall, her jaw clenched, her hands curled so tightly, her knuckles were white.

"She's psi," James barked.

Connor laughed. "I don't know what the hell that means, but she's more than that. She's Shadow Pack."

I gaped at him. Erin? That was impossible. Lana was Shadow Pack. I wasn't Shadow Pack—I couldn't enter and exit the Shadow Realm whenever I pleased, we'd all been witness to that. Which meant she couldn't be. There was plenty I didn't know about my parents, but Erin and I being connected by blood? That I was sure of.

Anger flared on James' face. "You're a liar."

"Ask her." Connor nodded to Lana. "She knows it's true. Which means even if Lana won't participate in this bargain, Erin will be able to take you into the Shadow Realm. If you stop the fire, if you let them go—I'll give you the dagger, and we'll get the book."

I sucked in a sharp breath. No. No, no, no—

Callista made a strangled noise, and I could see the wheels turning in all their heads. Lana. Destin. Callista. But one wrong move and Kael was dead. Gabriel—

I frowned. Where the hell was Gabriel? A moment ago, I could've sworn he was standing next to Destin. Hope bubbled through me. Maybe he was going to do something—appear out of nowhere, knock the dagger free.

I glanced up and Connor was staring directly at me. *Trust me.*

And suddenly, everything snapped into place. His questions in the Shadow Realm. Lana's explanation of how the dagger had been stopped, how the book was acquired. But what the hell was he talking about with Erin?

James tapped a finger against his chin. "And I'm just supposed to take you at your word? You, a human, who knows nothing of our kind?"

Connor's jaw locked. "I don't care what you believe. You want the relics? I'm giving them to you."

James studied him, then let out a low chuckle. "I think I'll make sure."

He strode forward and snatched the amulet, letting it catch the firelight. "This will bind you to that promise."

Connor's fingers tightened around the dagger. "Fine."

Panic flooded my veins, and my wolf rose through my consciousness. We could shift. I tried to push through her, but she barked in protest. She was still healing, still recovering from James ripping her out of my body.

James stalked forward, clutching the amulet with both hands.

He can't do this. He doesn't understand what the relics do. What they will take from him. My wolf howled within me.

Then a voice echoed in my mind. Soft. Strong. Unyielding. *She saved his daughter. So now he will save hers.*

My body froze. I knew that voice. My head whipped around, searching for Gabriel, but before I could process it— before I could even breathe—James held the amulet out.

In one swift movement, Connor dropped Kael and drew the dagger across his wrist. Not a shallow cut. A deep, deliberate slice. Blood poured over the blade, coating the metal, dripping onto the amulet.

A strangled cry dragged through me, my hands clutching at my chest. The relics pulsed, their power drinking him in, binding him. James stilled. The fire still burning around the clearing sputtered, recoiling.

And I felt myself break.

Connor staggered, his skin pale, blood dripping to the dirt. Lana gasped, her body jolting like she'd been struck. Destin caught her in his arms as Callista rushed toward Kael.

James' lips curled in delight, and Erin—

She fell from the wall, her whole body releasing like she'd been exorcised. She drew in a shaky breath and lifted her head, her eyes frantic. Clear. She looked like herself again. "He took the bond!" Erin stumbled forward, and her eyes locked on mine. "He can't handle it, Mia! It will—"

James yanked her up by her arm and dragged her over to where Connor stood, hunched over, still holding the dagger. James snatched it from his hands. "Take me. Now."

No. The word reverberated through me as heat flared deep in my belly. Shadow Pack, my ass. My sister wasn't taking James anywhere and Connor wasn't taking on any bond except for mine.

He couldn't handle the power of the amulet, but if Erin could, I could. My wolf surged, her desperation and fury finally focusing on a single point.

Connor.

I threw my consciousness forward, setting my wolf free. She burst forth, both of us ignoring the burning pain as I shifted. She wasn't healed, but neither of us thought about the risk. She flew across the floor of the hall, lunging at Connor and knocking him onto his back.

The dagger skittered across the tile, and my wolf lapped at

the blood spilling over his hand. Mine. He was mine. He would not die for me or my sister. He would not be punished for what he did not understand.

Connor was strong. He was good. He protected even when he shouldn't.

I didn't care if this bond took my magic. If I could never shift again or if I went mad. I'd found my sister, but I didn't save her. Connor did that.

The bond ignited, surging to life. I followed it. Dove into it.

It wasn't just magic. It was him, his strength, his stubborn, stupid, self-sacrificing heart.

And I wouldn't let him go.

CHAPTER

TWENTY-SEVEN

CONNOR

I woke in heaven. That was the only explanation.

The bed beneath me was impossibly soft, like it had been spun from clouds. The scent of pine and something sweet and earthy drifted through the air. Golden light filtered through a canopy of deep green leaves, dappling across my bare chest.

A forest. The trees stood impossibly tall, their trunks twisted like something ancient and wise. The air shimmered, alive in a way the real world never was.

I had died. And this was what came after.

A sigh escaped me, half relief, half resignation. At least it hadn't hurt. Not really.

I remembered the fire. The relics. The feeling of my blood pouring over the dagger and amulet, sinking into something deeper.

Regret stole through me. I didn't know how it ended. I'd given a willing, selfless sacrifice like Lana had said. It had worked for the dagger, but I didn't know if it would work for the amulet. I only hoped.

I pushed up to sitting and scanned the area around me, searching for swirling flames or smoke. Nothing.

My chest tightened. I needed to know what happened. I had to see whether the fire was contained, whether Erin and Mia—

My heart stopped in my chest, and I knew for sure I was dreaming. I'd thought her name, and there she was, standing in front of me.

Mia stood a few feet away, her dark hair tumbling down her back in loose waves, her eyes shadowed in thought. She looked untouched by death. Untouched by pain.

Vibrant. Healthy. She was so damn beautiful.

A new ache settled in my chest, one that had nothing to do with the fire. I'd wanted her. Hell, I still wanted her. And I never even got to tell her. But if this was heaven, I'd take what I could get. Even if it was only a dream.

She turned, her gaze landing on me. "Connor," she breathed, stepping closer.

My lips curved into a smirk, even as my heart twisted. "Either some God loves me or I'm about to be tortured for eternity."

Mia raised an eyebrow. "What would I do if some God loved you?"

My mouth went dry. I was about to say exactly what she'd do when I noticed another figure approaching. My eyes widened, and the words died on my tongue. I cleared my throat. "You're sister's here."

Mia smirked. "Is that a problem?" She sat next to me and as her thumb brushed mine, a jolt passed through me. I sucked in a breath, my entire body lighting up like a Christmas tree.

"What the hell was that?" I hadn't meant to snap, but I felt like a tree branch had just landed on my head and I wasn't wearing a hard hat.

Mia's cheeks flushed. "I—"

"Are you going to introduce me, or do I have to do it myself?" Erin stood at the foot of the bed, her arms crossed over her chest.

Mia tucked her hair behind her ear. "Ha, ha. You know Connor."

Erin gave a cheeky grin. "I know Connor as Elle's dad—"

"Okay, okay, this is Connor Bastien, the fire chief in Kitimat. And yes, he has a daughter, but he wasn't really that much older than us. We're only what, ten years apart?" She looked at me, flustered.

I grinned, my brows pinching. "Uh, yes, but—"

"Great." Mia slapped her hands on her thighs. "So, Erin, I think—"

"How are you feeling?" Erin grinned, plopping down on the bed.

I pushed myself up on my elbows, wincing at the ache in my limbs. Sore. I picked up my hand and saw a bandage there. My eyes narrowed. Did they have bandages in heaven?

I blinked at her, trying to make sense of everything. "I—" I swallowed. "Dead? Or am I not dead, because—"

Erin laughed out loud. "Decidedly not dead."

"Someone's going to be dead if they don't leave immediately," Mia murmured.

My mind was spinning too fast to catch any of it. I exhaled sharply, running a hand down my face. Dead would've been easier to believe. "So we're—"

"In the Shadow Realm." Mia stared at me like she thought I

might vanish. "After you used the dagger and the amulet, both of us got pulled here."

I frowned, my thoughts still too slow to catch up. "The Shadow Realm," I repeated.

She nodded. I looked around again, at the strange, glowing forest, at the way the air seemed to hum with magic. Okay. Sure. Why not. But something nagged at me. "Have you been here the whole time?" Mia nodded. "Which is?"

"Four days."

I sucked in a breath. Four days. I was instantly thinking about my team, about Tiff, about the fire. I moved, trying to throw my legs off the bed, but Mia blocked me. "Connor, you can't—"

"I need to get back to my crew. The fire—"

"Is contained." Mia beamed at me, and the breath whooshed from my lungs. She nodded as if to prove I could believe her.

"Then I need to get things organized. I—"

"Connor." Erin leveled a gaze at me. "You can't."

I sat up fully, my stomach tightening. "What do you mean I can't?"

Erin shrugged. "I tried to take you, but it wouldn't work. Lana said it was like that the first time."

"Because Mia needs to go with me."

"I tried," she admitted. "But something pulled us both back."

My chest tightened. Something about that felt . . . important. Like it should mean something. But I couldn't put my finger on it.

Erin and Mia shared a look.

"What?" I asked.

"Nothing," Mia answered too quickly.

"Mia—"

"She thinks this realm is keeping you alive," Erin answered, and Mia glared at her. "What? He deserves to know."

I swallowed. Hard. "So . . . you think I'm stuck here? And you—"

"Erin, can you please give us some privacy?" Mia's voice was no longer light and teasing.

Erin nodded once, then a shadow passed over her face. "You knew," she said, looking back at me.

I frowned. "Knew what?"

"That I was Shadow Pack."

I exhaled, more pieces dropping into place. "Lana and Destin were talking about passing memories. About how Shadow Pack can pass them between each other." I met Erin's gaze. "You passed yours to us. That night while you slept. And one of them—" I glanced at Mia, "—was the one Lana saw."

Mia looked completely floored. "When did you and Lana talk about what she saw?"

I blinked. "You heard it, too. When we were in the Shadow Realm the first time."

Mia looked puzzled, and then realization hit. Her face turned red. "I—" She pursed her lips. "I wasn't paying attention."

I raised a brow. "Huh. What was distracting you?"

She looked away, scowling.

Erin chuckled, shaking her head. "Guess I should be thanking you," she said.

I turned back to her, my amusement fading. "You don't have to thank me."

Erin exhaled, twisting her fingers. "You don't understand. That thing—it weighs on you. I was sleeping most of the time. Even James." She swallowed. "He was exhausted. Even though I was taking all of the weight, he could barely function some days."

A sick feeling curled in my stomach. "What happened? To the relics. To James."

Erin shifted, her gaze moving past me toward the trees. "Lana has them."

My eyebrows shot up. "All three?"

She nodded. "But James, I don't know. Destin did some damage, but one of the other alphas showed up, and with you injured and Mia . . ."She trailed off. "I should go," she murmured. Erin gave me one last look, then turned on her heel and disappeared into the mist.

And then it was the two of us. For a long moment, neither of us spoke.

Mia looked at me, her eyes searching mine, and suddenly, the weight of everything we had been through crashed down on me.

The fire.

The relics.

Her.

I had nearly died. Had given my blood to stop James, to save them. And all I could think about was that moment in the closet. How she'd turned her back and forced me to go.

"I'm going to tell you something," she said in a rush. I frowned, but before I could speak, she continued, "If you hate me, I'll understand."

My throat worked. "I don't think it's possible for me to hate you."

Mia grimaced. "Well, let's hold that thought.

CHAPTER
TWENTY-EIGHT

MIA

Connor was alive.

I had spent hours, maybe days, sitting at his side, waiting, willing him to wake up. To breathe. To open those infuriating, beautiful hazel eyes and look at me like he always did—like I was something he could figure out if he just tried hard enough.

Now he was here, in front of me, very much breathing, very much alive, and I didn't know how to feel.

Relief should have flooded me, but instead, my chest ached in a way that had nothing to do with fear.

I knew why. I hesitated, my fingers twisting in the blanket beneath me. How the hell was I supposed to say this?

The silence stretched too long.

Finally, he sighed. "Mia, spit it out."

I exhaled sharply, looking down at my hands. "When we were in the Shadow Realm before, I . . . I felt something."

Connor's expression didn't change. "Like what?"

Winced before the words were even out. "A connection. A bond."

His brow furrowed. "A bond?"

I nodded, not trusting myself to look at him. Connor wasn't a shifter. He didn't understand what that meant. I took a slow breath, gathering the words. "Shifters . . . we don't just choose a mate, Connor." I risked a glance at him. His jaw tightened slightly, but he didn't interrupt. "When we bond, it's forever." I wet my lips, forcing myself to keep going. "It's not like humans. We don't just fall in love and hope it works out. We feel it. It's . . . deeper. A physical and emotional tie that binds us together until we die and spiritually after."

Connor's eyes flickered, but he still didn't speak, so I kept going. "We don't take this lightly. Once we bond, we can't break it. It's permanent, and it's supposed to be with another shifter—"

Connor's gaze sharpened. "Supposed to be?"

I bit my lip. Shit. There it was, dangling between us, impossible to take back.

Connor sat up slowly, shifting so he was closer. His eyes searched mine, and I knew the exact second he realized what I was saying. "Mia," he said, voice low, rough. "Are you telling me . . ."

I forced myself to nod, even though every nerve in my body screamed for me to run.

His throat worked. "You think we—you and I—"

I swallowed. "It's not really theoretical. Not anymore."

Silence. It stretched too long, filling the space between us, making my chest tighten with dread. Then—

"How?" Connor's voice was too calm. "How is that even possible?"

I forced a breath. "It's not. Not exactly." His jaw clenched. I shook my head, trying to explain. "There have been cases—rare ones—where a wolf has bonded to a human, but it's dangerous."

He narrowed his eyes. "Dangerous, how?"

My throat felt tight, like the words were trying to choke me. "Wolves who bond with humans lose their magic."

His entire body went still. When I finally forced myself to look at him, I saw something dark flicker across his face. "Explain to me the 'not theoretical' part of this conversation."

I swallowed hard, my hands twisting into the blanket beneath me, my breath shallow as I stared at Connor. He was alive. He was here. And I had bonded him.

I hadn't thought twice about it. And I knew the consequences. A wolf who bonded with a human suffered for it. Our magic wasn't meant to be tied to something so fragile, something unchangeable.

A wolf's magic adapted, shifted, moved with the tides of life and the bond of the pack. But when we tethered ourselves to a human? It stripped us. Took everything that made us what we were.

And yet, when I saw him dying before my eyes, I'd made my choice.

"I bonded you," I confessed, my voice breaking. "I didn't have a right to. I didn't—" I swallowed hard, my throat aching. "I didn't ask. And because of that, it's not solid."

Connor blinked. "What does that mean?"

"It means the bond is volatile. It's not set. Not yet. Because I did it without your consent." Ugh, I groaned internally, dropping my head into my hands. It sounded awful. Predatory.

Connor exhaled, rubbing a hand over his face. "Okay," he said slowly. "Tell me what this actually means."

I exhaled, not willing to look at him. "I knew you couldn't handle whatever bond Erin had been holding. I felt the weight of it, and it was going to kill you. I couldn't let that happen."

He pinched the bridge of his nose between his thumb and forefinger. "But I don't have a wolf to bond."

"Right. I know. Wolves bond with their fated mate through their wolf and their human. It's not just a physical connection—it's emotional. Spiritual. We feel each other. Sense each other. Our magic and our instincts become one."

Connor wasn't breathing. I could see the way his chest barely moved, his eyes locked on me, taking in every word.

"So I bonded the physical piece. You. But as I said, it's unstable. Even working through half a bond—"

"How do we make it solid, then?"

My entire body flushed hot. I couldn't look at him. I couldn't say it.

Connor tilted his head. "Mia."

I shook my head, scooting back from him instinctively. "That isn't—we don't need to talk about that," I bumbled. "I think this whole thing might be why you can't leave the Shadow Realm, and you can choose to refuse it. You can let it go, we can pretend the whole thing never happened, and hopefully, you can go back to your own life—"

"Mia, can you shut up a second?" he pleaded. I looked up, snapping my mouth closed. Connor watched me, thinking.

And I saw it. The second he realized why I was being skittish. I didn't avoid talking about sex, but telling him I'd bonded him without consent and then telling him the only way to solidify that bond he didn't want was to have sex?

Connor's pupils dilated. His muscles tensed. The raw

energy and power of him seemed to expand, filling the space between us like a pulse of heat.

My wolf stilled. Connor hadn't even moved, but I could feel it. Hunger. Not just desire. Something darker. Deeper. Something primal.

I stood, my breath shaky. "I need to go. I need to give you time to think. You can't make this decision with the bond muddling your mind, and really, I'm fine if—"

"Mia. Stop."

Before I could react, he was moving. Fast. One second, I was scrambling off the bed. The next, his hands were on me.

He lifted me like he did in his trailer, plucking me off the ground and dropping me back onto the bed before I could even struggle.

Why in the name of Seraphina was that so damn hot?

Connor loomed over me, his expression dangerous. "Are we alone?"

I swallowed hard, nodding. "Yes."

His gaze searched mine. "Did you only bond me because you felt guilty?" I shook my head. "Because I was dying?"

Another shake. "No."

He exhaled slowly. "Why?"

I squeezed my eyes shut. My heart hammered.

"Because I love you." The words slid out on a breath. I hadn't meant to say it. Humans did not say I love you after knowing each other for a week. They didn't understand how fast a mating bond could snap into place, and Connor probably didn't feel anything close to what I felt on my end of the bond. He was going to think I was crazy.

Connor's entire body tensed. "Say that again."

"Connor—"

He pushed me onto my back, pinning my arms to the bed.

He dropped his head, pressing his cheek against mine like he had outside the window. "Say it again, Mia."

"I love you," I whispered in his ear.

Fingers trembling, I slowly slid my hands up his chest, feeling the heat of him, the strength beneath my palms.

"Am I correct in assuming that this physical bond would be strengthened if—"

"Mmhmm," I murmured. "But I don't want you to—"

He buried his face in my neck, his teeth catching my skin. I hissed air through my teeth.

"Don't want me to do what?" His voice rumbled through me as he clasped my wrists and lifted my arms over my head, kissing over my skin like he had in the closet. "Do you like it better when I'm on my knees?"

He moved down my body, lifting my shirt and pressing his cheek into the hollow of my stomach. I whimpered, dropping my hands to play with his hair. I loved his hair. Thick and unruly.

"You want this?" Connor asked, and I nodded.

"I don't know what it will mean."

Connor pressed his lips against my hip bone. "You could lose everything."

"I know. I knew that when I chose this."

Connor lifted his head, waiting until I met his gaze. "Do you still want to choose it."

I drew in a shaky breath. "Yes."

Connor snapped.

A growl ripped from his throat. Raw. Desperate. Uncontrolled. His breath was ragged, his fingers trembling where they clutched my waist, his entire body coiled and tense.

His mouth hovered just over mine. A silent question. A final warning. Are you sure?

Again, trying to protect me. Even from my own damn choices.

I answered the only way I knew how. I pressed my lips to his.

And Connor lost control.

TWENTY-NINE

CONNOR

M ia's lips were exactly how I imagined. Soft, insistent, intoxicating. Her touch seared through me, leaving fire in its wake, unraveling every tightly held piece of myself until I was bare and vulnerable beneath her hands.

I had spent years holding back. Years believing I wasn't enough. That I wasn't the kind of man a woman could truly love. That I had failed.

But here, with Mia beneath me, wrapped around me, whispering my name like a prayer, I felt whole.

She loved me. I'd bled for her, and she'd risked everything to keep me alive.

I kissed her harder, deeper, pushing past hesitation, past fear, past every doubt that had ever taken root inside me. Her hands slid down my back, nails dragging lightly, and something flipped within me.

A shift. A stirring. A surge of something primal.

The moment it hit me, I froze.

It wasn't just desire. It wasn't just the heat of our bodies, the way she molded against me so perfectly it felt like she had been made for me.

It was something more. Something older. Wilder. A growl rumbled deep in my chest, low and unfamiliar.

Mia gasped against my mouth, but she didn't pull away. She tightened her grip, pressed herself closer, welcoming it. Welcoming me.

My pulse hammered. My breath came ragged and uneven. I pulled back, staring at her, trying to understand. Was this what she was talking about? This physical bond? Was I sensing her layering through me?

Her eyes burned, full of heat, full of something deeper. Something unbreakable. And then she whispered, "Give in."

I shuddered at her words. She knew. She saw it. Felt it. Whatever this was.

A new voice sounded in my head, aggressive and possessive. "Mia—"

"I know. I hear you." She wanted it. *She wanted me.*

I crushed my lips to hers again, needing to drown in her, in this. Needing to lose myself completely. Her body arched beneath mine, perfect, warm, soft in all the ways that made my brain short-circuit.

I had never felt so strong. So alive. Every touch, every kiss, every breath between us was electric.

We undressed like two teenagers, throwing our clothes like free T-shirts at a hockey game. She whispered my name between gasps and moans, her hands gripping my shoulders, my arms, my back—like she was afraid I'd disappear.

"I'm not going anywhere." I kissed my way down her throat, across her collarbone, down the smooth curve of her stomach.

"You're so good, Connor. Please. Just let me feel you. You're so—" She sucked in a breath, and I slowed, waiting. I wanted her to keep talking. I couldn't hear enough.

"I still think about that night."

"What night?" I murmured against her thigh.

"When I slept in your bed. In the trailer."

I grinned. "I knew you were looking."

She let out a long sigh. "I was absolutely looking."

Slow was no longer an option. That force, that insatiable drive took control. She was perfect. Exactly right in an almost unbearable way.

It was as if I split down the middle. I wanted to take my time, to memorize every inch of her, but my instincts wouldn't let me.

That new, wild sensation screamed that I needed to claim her. To mark her, whatever the hell that meant. To make her mine in every way that mattered.

I had never wanted anything more.

Her hands tangled in my hair, her breath shaky, her body trembling beneath me. But she wasn't afraid. Not of me. Not of this.

She welcomed the bond she spoke of. The thought made something snap inside me. I kissed my way back up, capturing her mouth in a kiss so deep I felt it in my soul.

And then I couldn't wait another second. I nudged her thighs wide, and our bodies became one. I sucked in a breath, my entire body going rigid.

It was too much. Too perfect. I gritted my teeth, trying to hold on, to savor every second, but Mia rolled her hips against mine, and my self-control shattered.

I moved, drinking in every tiny gasp, every sharp intake of breath. Her hands still clawed at my back, dragging me closer.

"So good," she murmured, her tongue catching the lobe of my ear.

I leaned down, kissing her hard, my fingers lacing through hers as I pinned them above her head.

My instincts roared. Claim her. Mark her. She belonged to me.

I nipped at her throat, my teeth scraping over the sensitive skin, and she let out a sound that drove me insane.

Her scent wrapped around me, heady and intoxicating, making my vision blur with need. The pleasure built, twisting and curling, coiling too tight.

I could feel her spiraling with me. I could feel everything. The bond was no longer frayed, no longer volatile. It was solid. Whole. Ours.

I growled, low and deep, and sank my teeth into the curve of her shoulder. Mia cried out, her body locking against mine as she came undone beneath me. I followed, lost to the storm, to her, to the power surging between us.

The bond snapped into place.

Final. Permanent. Unbreakable.

I collapsed, feeling her clench around me. I didn't want to crush her, but I barely had the strength to roll us over, keeping her tucked against my chest.

She let out a slow, contented sigh, her fingers tracing nonsense shapes over my skin.

"How did you know how to do that?" she whispered.

"Which part?"

She laughed, swatting my ass. "The mark. You gave me one." She trailed her hand up to her shoulder.

I let out a long, shaky breath, my lips brushing against her hair. "I don't know."

"Connor, my wolf felt something—"

"I sure as hell hope so."

She grinned. "Can you be serious for five seconds?"

"Three. Maybe." I just had the best sex of my life. I didn't think I was going to be serious ever again.

She tilted her head so she could look at me, still holding herself tightly in place against my hips. "I think there's a chance that it wasn't just my bond. That you—"

She didn't finish her sentence. Because Gabriel appeared at the side of our bed.

THIRTY

MIA

A swirl of darkness appeared near the trees, coalescing into a familiar silhouette, and I shrieked. Connor swore, yanking the blankets over us.

I grabbed the closest thing I could find, which just so happened to be Connor's arm, and hid beneath it.

"What the hell?" I hissed at Gabriel from under Connor's shoulder.

He looked deeply unimpressed.

Connor's body shook with laughter above me. "Hey, bud. Ever heard of knocking?"

Gabriel sighed. "It's the Shadow Realm. I don't have a door to knock on."

I wanted to die. Right there. Just spontaneously combust.

Gabriel looked at Connor, completely unfazed by the fact that we were both naked under the sheets.

"You made a sacrifice to the amulet," he said bluntly. "And it was accepted."

I froze.

Connor stopped laughing. "What does that mean?"

A sacrifice. Connor had spilled his blood with the dagger, and the dagger hadn't come for him like it had Callista. There was still so much we didn't understand—so much we were learning as we went.

Were the relics truly satiated? I'd spent hours hashing it out with Lana, Destin, Kael, Callista, and Erin while Connor slept.

Were they returned to their original state? Or would they always carry a propensity for darkness? Magic always came at a cost. But they were forged to save the Shadow Pack. How could both be true?

Gabriel crossed his arms, but before we could get more information, another ripple in the air appeared, and suddenly, Lana, Destin, and Erin were standing there.

"Shit," Connor muttered.

Destin smirked. "Well, look at that. You two finally—"

"Do not finish that sentence," I snapped.

Lana cleared her throat, looking very much like she wanted to be anywhere else. "I was going to wait," she said flatly. "But we need to talk. Now."

Erin looked at Connor, her eyes darting to where I had my death grip on the sheet. Then she looked at me. Then back at Connor. "Seriously? When you said you wanted to be alone—"

"Erin!" I wanted to die all over again.

Lana sighed, rubbing her temples. "Look. It's done. And now we have a bigger problem."

Connor sat up, keeping the sheets pooled dangerously low on his hips. "It's done?"

Gabriel's voice was calm but firm. "You are bonded. You and your mate were adopted into the Shadow Pack."

Silence.

Connor cleared his throat. "Excuse me?"

I stared at Gabriel. I'd told Lana and Destin about what I felt here. Why I'd made the decision to save Connor's life.

But how was it possible? Adopted into the Shadow Pack. Connor. A human.

My hands began to tremble. What I'd felt, how my wolf had reacted a few moments ago, it was strong and deep and all-consuming. She'd felt something more than just a physical connection.

I was right. There was more between us than just a partial bond. I turned to Connor, my eyes pricking with tears.

Gabriel continued matter-of-factly, "You've been given a wolf. You'll start to feel him—"

"Oh, I feel him," Connor muttered, pinching my hip under the sheets.

I bit my lip. *Given a wolf?* The implications hit me like a sledgehammer.

Lana crossed her arms. "You're not just bonded to Mia. You're one of us now." Connor blinked. "Which means you have a lot to catch up on. As your alpha, I don't want you dragging your ass."

A slow smile spread across his face. "Can I do invisibility shit?"

Lana rubbed her temple. "That was the amulet, asshole. Your blood released that particular power."

Destin grunted. "I tried."

Lana grabbed his arm. "Look. You two take your time." I started to relax— "But not too much time. Tiff is wondering where the hell you are, we still have two relics to find, and we just got more intel on James and the alphas."

Connor exhaled. "Perfect. Can't wait for that conversation."

Lana sighed. "I'm sure Tiff will take the absence well."

"She won't."

"No, she won't."

Then, without another word, they all faded into the mist, leaving us blissfully alone. I let out a long, shaky breath, still trying to process everything.

Magic always has a cost. The thought pulsed through me, tinging my euphoria at the edges. Was it all magic? Mine? Connor's?

Connor kissed my forehead, settling back on his pillow. His skin was too warm, his hands still on me, like he wasn't wholly convinced that we weren't still in the middle of what just happened.

I couldn't think. Not about the fact that we had bonded. Not about the fact that he had a wolf. Not about the fact that I wanted him again already.

I blinked up at him, still stunned, still reeling, but all he did was grin. That cocky, insufferable grin. "I have a wolf."

"You have a wolf."

He traced the line of my shoulder. "I mean, I've always had a wolf—"

"Serious, remember?" I hissed.

Connor propped himself on an elbow, his tone pure mischief. "Oh, I agree. Very serious. But did you feel my wolf? Extremely deep inside you?"

I gaped. "Connor—"

"Wild, untamed, just waiting for the right moment to—"

"I swear to the gods, if you finish that sentence, I will kill you."

He laughed, unrepentant. "What? I just think it's a little unfair. You've had years to make wolf jokes, and I've had . . . " He pretended to think. "What, like, ten minutes?"

I dropped my face into my hands. "I hate you."

"Lies."

"I do. So much."

He dragged his lips over my jaw. "That's not what you said a few minutes ago." His voice dropped, teasing, warm, familiar. "Do you think there's a closet we could find around here?"

I blushed furiously. "And why do you want a closet?"

He lifted his face, still grinning from ear to ear. "Maybe you could put on my shirt."

My jaw dropped. "Connor, we were in a very dire situation and you were fantasizing?"

"Fantasizing came after the fact."

I slapped his shoulder, and he rolled over me, threading his legs with mine. "I'll pick you up and set you wherever you want. I'll get on my knees. I'll beg you to forgive me—"

My eyes rolled back in my head. "For what this time?"

"Anything you want."

When I laughed, he caught my face in his hands, his expression sobering. "Mia."

"Connor."

He exhaled. "I won't be good at this. You'll have to teach me."

"I'm a good teacher. I give out gold stars and everything." I ran my finger over his jaw. "I'm worried you won't want this. That you're going to find out more and wish—"

Connor put a finger to my lips, then brushed his nose against mine. "I love you." My heart skipped a beat. "I knew it the second you refused to eat my microwaveable food." I laughed again, this time deep and in my belly. "Actually, it was the second Liam patted your knee."

My eyes flew wide. "You noticed that?"

He nipped at my skin. "Mia."

"Connor."

He blew out a breath, and my skin prickled. "I'm not going to change my mind."

My heart sped. "Even if you can't stay in Kitimat?"

"I can visit, can't I?"

I nodded. "What about Elle?"

He paused a moment. "Elle is an adult. I love her. We'll find a way."

I nodded. "And what if our duties are dangerous?"

He raised an eyebrow. "Mia—"

"Okay, yeah. I know your answer on that one."

Connor kissed over my collarbone, then ran his thumb over my skin where he'd marked me.

I tried to look but couldn't see it clearly. "What is it?"

Connor's voice was low and soft. "What do you think it is?"

I didn't even have to take a guess. Because right then, my entire body went up in flames.

EPILOGUE

ERIN

I should have felt relief going home.

The wind carried the familiar scent of pine and salt, the crisp bite of the ocean air rolling in from the bay. The streets hadn't changed, and the mountains still loomed in the distance.

But I felt like a stranger.

Coming back to Kitimat after so many years away felt like stepping into someone else's life. The girl who had once belonged here—who had laughed in this town, played in these forests, run through these streets as a wolf—

She wasn't me anymore.

Mia held my hand as we stood in front of our childhood home, my heartbeat a frantic rhythm in my chest.

The house was exactly as I remembered. The same dark wood panels. The same porch swing swaying in the wind. The same front door I had walked out of years ago, never expecting to come back.

Through the window, I saw my mother's silhouette. And suddenly, my throat closed. I wasn't ready.

Mia squeezed my fingers. "You don't have to do this today."

I nodded, but I knew the truth. If I didn't do it now, I never would. So I took a breath and stepped inside.

THREE DAYS LATER, Shadow Pack—all five of us—and members of the other southern packs had moved up north. We weren't talking about any of it yet. The relics, the Shadow Realm, or my time with James.

I wasn't ready. I didn't know if I ever would be.

More than that, I still didn't understand how Shadow Pack was in my blood, and none of us had any time to dig deeper.

The fire had left scars. Blackened trees, scorched earth, the faint, lingering scent of smoke in the wind. We were working with the people whose homes had been lost, rebuilding, organizing supplies, offering support in the aftermath of the devastation.

Now we stood together, side by side, passing out water and blankets, guiding people to temporary shelters. Mia and Connor couldn't keep their hands off each other. Understandable, even if I was a little jealous.

"Mia, hurry the hell up," Liam barked. Mia laughed and picked up the box she was carrying after pausing to plant a kiss on Connor's cheek.

Liam was doing remarkably well with everything, considering. As was Tiff. They were adjusting nicely to being support people for others after losing their best friends.

I'd come to love Tiff over the past week. I left Black Lake

and Kitimat with a sour taste in my mouth. Now I wondered if part of the blame landed on me.

Mia found me across the room and winked. I winked back. It had been so long since I'd let anyone close. Since I'd let myself belong.

Kitimat Pack had never been mine. And yet, standing here among my friends—Connor talking to Rowan, Lana and Destin hammering together a shelter, Kael and Callista securing food for the displaced—I had found something I didn't realize I was missing.

Trash duty. Mia's voice sounded in my head. Okay. So there were some things I had enjoyed living without.

I grabbed a stack of empty boxes and walked them behind the building to the recycling dumpster. Right as I threw them in, a flicker of something strange curled in my stomach.

Not pain. Not exhaustion. Something else.

I paused, pressing a hand to my chest. It was subtle, but there—a shift. Like something inside me had moved since the moment the amulet's compulsion had been stripped away.

I frowned. I had spent so many months under James's influence that I hadn't stopped to wonder, what had I become without it?

The work continued, everyone moving together like a well-oiled machine. People were hurt. Lost. Some had no idea what had caused the fire.

We couldn't tell them, so we helped where we could, offering warmth, safety, anything to hold onto while they processed what had happened.

I carried supplies to a group of women setting up a makeshift kitchen, watching as Mia worked beside them, laughing, comforting, listening.

She had always been like this. Open. Giving. Stronger than

anyone realized. I wondered if I had ever been like that. I wondered if I could be again.

That night, after the sun dipped below the horizon and the air grew cold, Mia and I sat together on the hood of a truck, staring out over the darkened trees. Neither of us spoke. For a long time, it was just the wind and the sounds of the group settling for the night.

Mia exhaled, "It's good to have you back."

I swallowed hard, and guilt sat heavy in my chest. I had left her. Left our family. I didn't deserve her kindness, her trust.

But still, she gave it freely like she always had.

LATER THAT NIGHT, I stood in my cabin, brushing my teeth, exhaustion settling into my bones. I crawled into bed, flicking off the lamp and closed my eyes for sleep.

It didn't take long for everything to shift. The world around me vanished, and I was somewhere else.

The disorientation hit like a freight train. The scent of smoke, leather, blood. The weight of power dark and ancient, pressing against my ribs.

The scene unfolded like a nightmare. James sat at a massive stone table, the goblet in front of him, its surface shimmering like liquid night.

The other alphas surrounded him, waiting. Watching. The goblet shimmered as James lifted it to his lips.

"You should not be here," a low voice sounded next to me, and I jumped. Before I could cry out, a hand clamped over my mouth. "Quiet. Or he'll hear you."

My eyes darted as I clutched my hand over his, struggling to breathe.

The vision broke. I gasped awake, sweat dripped down my spine.

My hands shook.

The goblet was real and it was in James' possession.

And someone knew I'd seen it.

🔥 *TROPES:*

✔ *Reluctant allies to lovers*
✔ *Training together*
✔ *"I can handle it" – "Not alone, you can't"*
✔ *Only he can pull her back from the darkness*
✔ *One bed... and an unbreakable rule*

ALSO BY LUNA M. ROSE

ABOUT THE AUTHOR

 Luna masquerades as a well-adjusted, functioning adult, but she secretly still believes in magic and wild things hidden just beyond the veil of our world. She has a fairy garden (with lights!) and lives with her husband and children near the Rocky Mountains in Colorado. She adores shiny objects.

www.ingramcontent.com/pod-product-compliance
Lightning Source LLC
Chambersburg PA
CBHW021709190726
48289CB00008B/2444